Unfinished Business

Unfinished Business

Michael Bracewell

WHITE
RABBIT

First published in Great Britain in 2023 by White Rabbit,
an imprint of The Orion Publishing Group Ltd
Carmelite House, 50 Victoria Embankment
London EC4Y 0DZ

An Hachette UK Company

1 3 5 7 9 10 8 6 4 2

Copyright © Michael Bracewell 2023

A CIP catalogue record for this book is
available from the British Library.

ISBN (Hardback) 978 1 3996 0439 0
ISBN (eBook) 978 1 3996 0441 3
ISBN (Audio) 978 1 3996 0442 0

Typeset by Born Group
Printed and bound in Great Britain by Clays Ltd, Elcograf S.p.A.

www.whiterabbitbooks.co.uk
www.orionbooks.co.uk

Prologue

I now introduce a black-and-white photograph, taken in the autumn of 1978.

The subject is my friend Francesca's boyfriend at that time, name of Martin Knight, with whom, as was her custom, she was briefly infatuated to the exclusion of all else. Francesca, then just turned eighteen (I was nearly twenty) and in the first flush of romance, took the photograph herself. Location: the long, overgrown garden of her parents' house in Wimbledon.

I recall the happy delight with which she crouched down to focus the camera, changing position to get different angles and between shots smiling encouragingly up at her beloved – who was seated, barely daring to breathe, on a precariously flimsy folding garden chair.

But love or luck imbued the portrait with an undeniable sense of presence. The top button of his white shirt unfastened, this latest beau has loosened what I remember to be an antique silver-grey tie, flecked with pinpoints of pink silk thread. Beneath stylishly cut black hair his young face is still soft-skinned and smooth-jawed; his nose is straight and his lips rather too red. The look in his dark-brown eyes is watchful and uncertain, almost fierce.

In what they hoped to be the style of a matinee idol, there is a lighted cigarette between the middle and index fingers of Martin's left hand – that rests lightly, thumb on high cheekbone, fingertips just touching his left eyebrow, as he inclines his head to one side. Smoke rises in languid coils. It is a successful study of indolent pose, either despite or because of the sitter's self-consciousness, which defined him.

Martin was a little younger than me but seemed much younger. Francesca had told me, protectively I felt, that he wrote poetry. He was eager to please and eager to impress. The way he conducted himself was like a succession of beginnings – hopeful shots at the world that resembled offerings or auditions.

Forty years ago the road ahead seemed to draw us steadily on towards real life. I was glad to get away, and so was Francesca. Not long after that she left for Russia – adventurous, even in those days – and I became a psychiatric nurse.

I have no idea what happened to Martin. I don't suppose I'll ever see him again.

One

On an overcast January morning in the year 2017 a man was waiting to cross Cambridge Heath Road. White sky over the interminable sprawl of East London. Behind him, in the cold flat light, the shuttered Venus Sports Bar looked as though it had been locked and empty for years.

He was still handsome. His dark hair was silvering at the sides, lending him a mildly distinguished air. He was reasonably but not noticeably tall; his jawline and features had kept their definition. His tired eyes held an expression that was both sorrowful and aloof – wary, perhaps.

His name in full was Martin Graham Crispin Knight. He was fifty-seven years old.

He was wearing a black overcoat, faded black leather gloves – one of which he was holding in his left hand – and a black scarf. His ageing dark suit, black lace-up shoes, white shirt and nondescript tie pronounced him a lifer in the service of office work.

Across the busy junction he could see the dimly lit entrance to Cambridge Heath station. The lights changed; and slowly, as though with effort, he started to cross the road.

The platform was reached by two steep flights of covered stairs. Martin looked up from the dirty bare subway that was open behind him to the street and morning traffic, and then he began to climb.

Such cramping and burning in his legs and feet! Like flame-hot iron shoes that tightened with each step. Vascular disease, *claudication* . . .

Only walking might improve the condition while only resting relieved the pain . . .

Twenty years ago, he and Marilyn – then still his wife – had taken their seats, quiet and scared, in a white office in a private hospital. The consultant sat sideways to his desk, florid beneath an aristocratic mop of silver hair.

'And you must ask yourself,' said the great man, 'do you prefer smoking to staying alive?'

The smartly dressed couple sat very still.

'I do not see an unsullied horizon,' he went on, studying the file. 'You are extremely young.'

Martin's narrowed aorta was reopened.

He gave up smoking, eventually. It had felt like the end of his youth.

With compromised arteries he struggled visibly on his commute. Forced to pause he would watch busy women hurrying to work; and men two decades his junior, lean and focused, striding towards their day.

Now, holding on to the banister, he hauled himself up the stairs to the platform. Finally he reached the top, breathless, his legs hurting. But immediately the air seemed fresher and the daylight brighter. An immense vista surrounded him. He was filled with a sense of calm. This was his favourite part of the day.

He often recalled how not so long ago, this whole area – Dalston, Kingsland Road, Mare Street, Hackney Central – had been desolate, haunted equally by boredom, poverty and menace. Melancholy parades of decrepit shops, wire mesh nailed over their windows; broad, apathetically littered streets, eerily empty. Murder Mile. Rotting old picture palaces and deserted parks. Silent estates; a few Victorian churches of extravagant design, mostly shut and shabby.

The elevated stretch of the line ran straight from Liverpool Street, just a few minutes away, through Bethnal Green and Cambridge Heath. Most weekday mornings, watched over by blocks of new apartments with neat balconies and windswept roof terraces, Martin surveyed the changing landscape.

The latest flats with their big windows; a glimpse within of brushed-metal worktops and pale wooden furnishings. To one side a long-abandoned warehouse, open to the sky. The weathered red brick was crumbling, sprouting scrawny shrubs.

It was like a middle-distant future, quiet and grey.

But even – what? Ten, fifteen years ago . . . in the lobby of the twenty-first century, which did not feel like his century – would you stand up here alone? At

5

any time of day? Or *thirty-seven* years ago? York Hall Baths, Old Ford Road.

Martin walked to the low bench and sat down more heavily than he had expected. He was alone, he noticed, at seven minutes past nine on that chill midwinter morning, aware of the pain subsiding in his legs, the working day to get through and the vast white sky.

It had been like this for the last few years. His job and rented flat. He had left the rooms rather bare but liked the view from the long kitchen window.

So many summers and sunsets; fleeting epiphanies, a marriage, working weeks, familiar streets, resentments, sudden panics, regrets, nurtured desires. All slipping slowly away, almost as though they had never happened. Just his daughter, Chloe – and she was in her twenties now, dark-haired, pretty, living her own life.

He felt a sudden swell in his sea of tranquillity. For recently, he fancied, he had become aware of an overview – a symptom of age, no doubt; his life presented to him as though by destiny, with an unnerving and unexpected shrug – '*There you go, then*' – dismissive, final.

So he reminded himself that there had been births and deaths, loss and love. A life of everything and nothing, during the six decades since he had opened his eyes to asphalt.

Beyond the suburbs of his boyhood, built to follow the railway lines, had arisen: shopping, television, pop, debt, aerobics, irony, computers, phones and coffee

shops that looked like Prohibition-era grain stores.
Then bigger things – climate change, terrorism – that
always seemed far away.

Like the suburbs, Martin had grown in step with the
London railway network; his earliest adulthood spent
in the old commuting world of overhead wires and
grey metal gantries, humming cables and black-oiled
tracks; damp waiting rooms that smelt of gas; broken
windows and empty subways.

Against such a backdrop he had sought first beauty
and then love. To him they were the same thing.

Now, this cold morning, he would take a train to
Liverpool Street to go to work.

He sat with his legs stretched out. He had got
heavier: the thickening process of late middle age –
'so *manly*,' an American woman visiting the office had
said. Women still found him attractive. 'You've *lived*!'
one had said not so long ago, mockingly, to flirt.

Behind him, in pale silhouette, Canary Wharf – the
plain blocks of dust-grey towers; to the right, closer, the
glinting curves, cones and rhomboid shapes of the City.

Some clouds had parted, revealing the pale disc
of the low winter sun. Standing, Martin could see
back streets and a bus depot; further off, the exposed
concrete stairwells on the side of some flats; a Somali
drop-in centre with crazily punched security glass.

In a broadsheet supplement interview, some
months earlier, the subject – an ageing French fashion
designer – had been asked: 'Your greatest regret?' And
responded: 'Nicotine.'

Martin had noted the answer and felt buoyed for a second. There was a satisfaction in searching through time's files for the start of his addiction to cigarettes. For that, in many ways, had been the start of everything.

It had begun one quiet afternoon when he was fifteen years old, at home in Thornby Avenue, kneeling in front of the sitting room fireplace.

In his mind's eye he saw the smooth black tiles of the hearth, dotted with soot; the brass-claw fire tongs and sabre-handled poker; the elongated decorative brick surround. It was a late spring day, almost summer. The fire was not laid; rain had brought the soot down. His father was still alive. And then he had smoked his first cigarette.

But how could such a significant event have occurred so quietly?

He had been with a school friend who was hesitant and slightly disgusted. For Martin the love affair with tobacco had been immediate and all-consuming.

Cigarettes, he believed, gave confidence, enlightenment and more; smoking was the enabler of pose and emblem of the aphoristic life, worldly glamour, rebel attitude.

What next in the old files, from memory's cavernous registry? To Tiles, a boarding school for boys in Kent.

In those days – 1975, '76 – during the summer holidays, Martin would select a day or wake inspired, dress in his best clothes and wait in warm sunshine for the heavy, acrid-smelling suburban train. Slam doors and luggage racks of knotted string netting. With a carnation in his buttonhole he would travel up to London to do three things.

First, to walk down Piccadilly, past the Ritz, the Burlington Arcade, the Royal Academy, Fortnum & Mason and Simpsons, to 34 Haymarket. Here stood a Georgian double bow-fronted shop, historically for nobility and gentry: Fribourg & Treyer, manufacturers of snuff and purveyors of tobacco products.

Number One Filter de Luxe was Martin's preferred brand, sold in a flat box of dove-grey card, embossed with black and gold.

Came a humid afternoon, around that time, when Martin would watch entranced as lovely Fenella – a teenage brunette Monroe, to him; his first love, painfully unrequited – weighed the pleasingly heavy box in her soft young palm; then held it up, admiring it. They were sitting on the patio at his childhood friend Christine's house; the heat-heavy garden; the neatly mown lawn before them.

Second, tea for one at the Ritz Palm Court. Young Martin, with his broad-lapelled checked sports jacket, oyster-beige Oxford bags, fat-knotted satin-style copper-gold tie, silver cigarette case and amber cigarette holder, had been led to his table with utmost seriousness by the tall, rigidly dignified maître d'hôtel.

Framed by mirrors, gilt and marble, the young aesthete had ordered Darjeeling tea, lit a cigarette and imbibed his setting like a drug.

And thirdly, to stroll to the dim-lit bar of the Café Royal and order there the cocktail of champagne and blue curaçao, upon the surface of which floated a single scarlet rose petal; name, redolent of the times: 'Suggestion of Something Special'.

The barman had liked him, overlooked his age and played up to the game of his pose as one of the indolent elect. Fed plenty of 'sir's and flattering attention, the teenage boulevardier had felt sure that the enfolding, shadowy bar was his rightful milieu; the suburbs far off and in those circumstances unmentionable – unthinkable, even.

Cigarettes had bound that world together and deepened its allure; were its communion and manifesto. Egyptian flats, Turkish, jasmine-scented, Virginia Nos. 1 and 2, Sullivan & Powell, Sobranie Cocktail, French Boyards, soft-pack Pall Mall and Russian even, Cossack brand – a short charge of bitter black tobacco, packed in diaphanous tissue at the end of a coarse cardboard tube.

Cigarettes from the days of imperial Europe and exotic Asia.

Smoking had offered a home, an aesthete's retreat – even back at Tiles. Martin, on the elevated platform, saw again winter daylight, the old school changing room's wooden floor, sodden with decades of water and mud, pitted by a century of boot studs.

This was where the smokers smoked. He had been one of two ostentatious smokers, with their arcane brands and snow-white shirt collars; their cigarettes held just so, to enable an insolently exquisite drag and pout.

One day, very early on – 1973, '74 – Martin had happened to glimpse into one of the small senior studies on the ground floor of a cold and gloomy boarding house. It was late afternoon, wintry and bleak. A foreboding bank of gunmetal cloud pressed down on the line of white-gold sunset, far off on the horizon.

In the study were two sixth-form boys, their dullish thick brown hair worn as long and unkempt as possible. One wore a naval greatcoat over his uniform, fully buttoned. The other, stock-still, was dressed in a three-piece college suit of grey serge, a broad black-and-white scarf around his neck.

Looking more carefully posed than casually seated – one in the wreckage of an armchair – both were staring silently ahead, seemingly at nothing, as though in a trance; and both were smoking, unblinking, with exaggerated refinement.

Each held his cigarette pushed down low between the index and middle fingers of the left hand, which was then brought gently to the left corner of the mouth. Inhale briefly with lips slightly parted, then pull the cigarette away from the mouth in a single staccato gesture – an abbreviated flick to the side. Exhale as though blowing lightly but sharply on a candle flame.

Behind them in the fading light, to the height of the ceiling, was an uninterrupted collage of overlapping posters: *Dirty Harry*, a cartoon cat with swastika eyes, Jimi Hendrix; a bare-breasted ash-blonde girl, hand on hip, denim hot pants – her accessories a beaded headband and automatic rifle.

From a brace of home-made speakers, impressively loud, The Mothers of Invention accompanied the falling dusk.

Unnoticed, Martin had been in awe of it all.

A little over a decade later, when he and Marilyn were taking his books out of cardboard boxes – their move to Bristol – she had looked in horror at the smoke-stained covers. *The King of Elfland's Daughter*, *Catch-22*, *Lolita* – the colour of tobacco juice.

Marilyn, to Martin, had been defined by fragrant cleanliness: pristine, unblemished – a trace of fern, bergamot, iris. He recalled a snowy night in January 1984.

The interior of Marilyn's smart black car had been filled with her lightly metallic floral perfume. To Martin it was the scent of sophistication and the modern life. This was their first journey together – the drive from Chiswick to Vauxhall – to Martin's first flat. Everywhere so quiet, a little after midnight, with freshly fallen snow; the shadowy bulks of tall dark buildings passing by.

It was as though they had the dimly luminous silent streets, the whole of London, to themselves. How she had enchanted him with her reserve – her seemingly cool pragmatism.

Now everything was wrong. Perhaps it had only needed one false step. In doing so badly at school, for instance, flailing in fervent adolescence? Had those exchanged confessions with Christine, forty years ago

– her teenage bedroom a shrine to romance, Mucha prints and Donna Summer; their pursuit of the new and confrontationally flamboyant, of heeding the call of heightened emotion above all – urged him down the wrong path completely?

His commonplace talents – mathematics, doing well in interviews for jobs – were, he felt, so at odds with his soul. He was a poet manqué, he had told himself. From that, clearly, all else proceeded . . .

After the divorce – and that was fourteen years ago now – Martin used to meet Stuart for dinner. They had known one another in the old days. Stuart was the former boyfriend of a school friend of Marilyn's called Catherine. In fact, Martin had first met Marilyn at Catherine's flat in Chiswick.

'Nowadays we'd call it depression,' Stuart had said about Catherine's sudden silences.

The two men would go to a busy fish restaurant in the shadow of Southwark Cathedral.

Here there was an exposed kitchen, fierce heat, sudden bursts of flame and noisy sizzling. The clamorous din of a newly opened brasserie. Chefs chucked halved lobsters onto spitting sheets of hot oil. Muscular renegade cooking was in fashion. Handfuls of salt, coarse-ground nuggets of black pepper, huge fistful squeezings of lemon and lime. More sizzling; lobster and chips with tamarind aioli. Martin had watched the things still twitching.

'It's the kind of place,' he had remarked to Stuart, 'where you have to be drunk already.'

Stuart had caught the waitress's eye and with a meaningful glance raised the bottle an inch.

'Same again?' she smiled, defining an epoch.

Good-natured Stuart had married an alcoholic psycho-therapist in Roehampton but was now separated again.

'I never knew a relationship counsellor who could throw up in the bath *during* a dinner party! Classic!'

He had been a good drinking companion. Quick to laugh, reserved yet amusing. Plump, owlish, he wore glasses with thick black frames. Sometimes he laughed so readily that Martin wondered whether he was simply very naive.

Then Stuart disappeared. Joined AA. Went daily to meetings in a crypt on Bishopsgate – packed, every one of them.

And Martin had walked the cold street from Bank station up towards Moorgate, alone.

He had sat on a bench near the Royal Exchange, leaning forward with his arms crossed tightly over his chest, rocking and blissful. A wonderful gale was blowing in his head. It was most important to get another drink.

Then, suddenly, the thought of religion had seemed ineffably brilliant and moving to him.

He imagined Oxford. Gothic Revival; a Christmas tree decked with playing cards.

And suppose he *had* got there, to Oxford, as he was meant to at Tiles?

But Fenella had taken him to South Kensington, one warm summer evening, all the way from Thornby

14

Avenue and innocently corrupted him, utterly without guile. In less than an hour she had shown him a world beyond the suburbs, beyond the ambitions he had lived with thus far.

He saw it through the big windows of Onslow Square drawing rooms. The low-shaded lamps and lazily extravagant cushions and Italian light fittings and significant paintings over the fireplace.

Scarlet brake lights flared softly in the blue Chelsea dusk.

It was like a midsummer magic, busily at work in the heady fragrant air.

And then he had to go all the way home again.

Decades later, in a pizza restaurant, alone, finishing a bottle of Chianti, he imagined the other life: 'My Oxford Years'.

Autumnal mists, moisture on high flinty walls, candle-lit medieval windows; deer parks, choristers, blossom, evensong and cloisters. Dust-filled sunbeams falling on ancient volumes . . . Modest yet confident young men, intellectually well bred. Girls of rare intensity from tumbledown aristocratic homes, part muse, part siren.

And they would all have had *fine minds*. That is, be able to order knowledge neatly and efficiently; and then be able to walk across Iraq − or similar − fine-mindedly; finding meaning and interest in a way that above all their fine-minded elders would approve of.

Which, being in a world of his own, Martin could never do. He knew that he not only lacked the right qualities but repelled those who had them. Now, where had he seen that exact same expression of sudden disgust before? Yes! On the face of the friend by the hearth, with their first cigarette each – not just the taste but the act. The two things that Martin had found so intoxicating.

Warm in the arms of alcohol, London Wall, at the pizza restaurant they had up there: glass walls, straddling the road; you could just sit by the window, above the traffic, surrounded by towers of concrete and glass, ice-blue-lit but deserted; and drink Chianti by yourself and get drunk and see meaning and poetry in every dark City doorway.

And now Martin was on the platform awaiting the nine twenty-seven. This had been his favourite part of the day. Everything and nothing. The avenues of plane trees at London Fields and Hackney Downs.

His life these days was circumscribed by the long streets with their little supermarkets, closed-down security firms, artisan coffee shops, weird conversions, steep steps up to big old houses, pristine new apartments, race-walking junkies and ageing estates. Still the Victorian churches were there, the missions and institutes; their mouldering walls topped with barbed wire and broken glass, some now with cosmically liturgical names.

And young families he would never know, susceptible to allergens and dust and gluten. Bearded dad and busy mum; their bikes, kids, coffee and computers.

How was it possible that he, Martin Knight of Cambridge Heath station and Hackney Central, had once lived in Bristol? The Flapjack Years. That had been his post-divorce joke about provincial life.

But even now, sometimes, if by chance he remembered somewhere quite ordinary they used to visit there, he would feel ashamed, and filled with sadness.

August 1989. The walk up the hill to Clifton, to their stately home in miniature: their big flat on the first floor of Ash House, with the view of St Mary Redcliffe that Marilyn had liked to point out to dinner guests. At her most charming, with her broad, delicious smile – her lustrous bobbed hair phase, red lipstick – she would explain that they would have to crane their neck, just a little, to the left . . .

On summer evenings, the three broad sash windows open. The warm lilac dusk and chestnut trees in blossom.

Going to their big wide bed, with fresh white Egyptian cotton sheets, violet- and lavender-scented. The pearl-coloured duvet cover chosen by his quiet, lovely, elegant wife. Then Ash House had felt like a magical galleon, setting sail to voyage through the night.

The eight coaches of the train arrived, still busy. The air brakes gave out their abrupt hiss and the doors slid open with a brief low rumble.

Expressionless passengers alighted.

Everyone looks like they live in Berlin, thought Martin.

In his old black suit, black shoes and black overcoat, he sat down slowly on the low warm cushions in a carriage that smelt of hot dust.

His hands in his coat pockets, he looked through a brownish stain on the carriage window. He saw an empty building, modern fifty years earlier, that looked as though all its windows had just been blown out. Then a brewery turned into a coffee shop and the rusted iron exoskeleton of an old gasometer. In a side street an elderly man with grizzled hair was talking to himself. He held a red plastic bucket and a handwritten sign: 'Hope Car Wash'. Then more new flats, these ones called 'art/Haus'.

It was a short journey, barely ten minutes. Martin always wished it lasted longer.

But forty years ago – yes, life had centred around the ashtray.

Nearing Liverpool Street, the passengers roused themselves for the tasks and further journeys ahead. As if reawakening, the men lost their inward gaze and re-entered the day. Young women hauled heavy tote bags to their shoulders, bracing themselves, looking around.

Martin did not join them. Only when the carriage was empty did he stand – pushing down hard on the tops of his legs, his left knee complaining against the strain. Then he walked slowly to the open train doors and stepped carefully down to the platform. In the distance, the drug wisdom of adverts flashed on digital billboards.

The drama of the station's roof never failed to catch his eye. The many columns that supported its vast span spread out at their tops like a jungle canopy made of peeling blue- and grey-painted ironwork.

As he walked down the platform he had the sense of approaching the west window of a cathedral, the sun blazing through. Or it might have been an orientalist fantasy of an antique temple-palace, built on water, with odalisques and water lilies. Looking up, he half expected to see jostling ripples of light on the underside of the roof.

The sight was ceremonial to Martin, as he strolled through the busy morning crowds, his hands in his overcoat pockets or held lightly behind his back.

With only partial irony, mimicking the steely certitude with which a young general, supernaturally gifted, might cross enemy lines in broad daylight, he would daily utter the part boast, part incantation: 'I am invisible!'

Two

Marilyn Fuller had never taken her husband's surname; and she had never felt at ease within her family. Her clever, distinguished parents; Carmen, her older sister – so outgoing and popular.

Now, this Sunday lunchtime – the last Sunday of January 2017 – Marilyn was standing with Catherine in the kitchen of her parents' pretty house in North London. The expensive simplicity of a Regency villa on a hill.

Bill and Josephine Fuller were elderly now. As regards their pretty house – to this situation their younger daughter was oblivious. She had only ever known good taste.

Reminded of his eightieth birthday, her father had decreed, 'Well, just a few old friends.'

Bill's first film, *Two Lives*, was reckoned a classic of socialist-realist cinema; his later documentaries for television – three in all – routinely claimed to fearlessly uphold the values of the Free Cinema movement, indurate to changing fashions. And thus Bill himself had become fashionable, then venerated; and hence the Sunday-lunchtime drinks party, at which the few old friends had become a sizeable crowd.

Marilyn was drinking soda water and blood orange, mixed with fresh mint and ginger. This was called a 'Cellini', apparently. Catherine held a glass of white wine. The sound of conversation and laughter from the library and drawing room grew louder.

The two women were both tired. They agreed that it had seemed like a long week; that the winter felt endless. Marilyn, now fifty-four, was older than her friend by just two months.

Despite having known her since their schooldays, Catherine still felt dowdy and unexciting when she was with Marilyn. For as long as she could remember, Marilyn had seemed almost perfect to her. Reticent but assured; so stylish and good-looking – with a presence, a beauty even, that had deepened over the years, like spring becoming summer.

Catherine found it hard to imagine that her old school friend had ever felt foolish or plain.

Marilyn had been told many times, over the years, that she had a lovely smile. The compliment had become a burden. It was tiring to have to look so pleased, so often, because people liked her smile.

Not so long ago she had started seeing an older man, wealthy, whose name Catherine could never remember. Thomas? Tobias? He lived in Brussels; little more than an outline that Catherine imagined was filled with glamour, companionship of a sort, and sex, presumably.

Marilyn seldom spoke about the relationship. When she did, she seemed to be trying to deny its significance.

Now Catherine was telling her about work; another divorce . . . Something about Brazil . . .

'—and just pack up and go. Which is what I would have done.'

Marilyn nodded and tried to concentrate. She glanced into the corridor, where Chloe was standing.

Chloe's dark hair was parted down the middle to frame her pale face with heavy brown ringlets. She had an intent, slightly startled air that brought to mind the countenance of a Victorian doll; and was dressed so correctly in high-waisted navy-blue trousers with a dulled silver buckle at the back; a cream shirt beneath a navy cashmere jumper. Black brogues.

Now twenty-six, she shared a house – a rather nice house, actually – with some friends of her own age in Putney. She and her friends were all very busy, all of the time. Their shared and all-consuming project – so it seemed – was their amazing lives.

A tall red-haired girl with a high short fringe had just put her hand on Chloe's shoulder and was laughing, her eyes shining . . . It took Marilyn a moment to place her. But it was Alice, of course. Alice who had gone to art school somewhere. An art girl.

She felt a faint weight on her thoughts that she recognised as boredom.

'I'm not sure I ever met him . . .' she said to Catherine, about someone her old friend had just mentioned. She had only been half attending.

'Well, I'm sure he said he knew Martin – or used to know him.'

As she spoke there was uncertainty in Catherine's pale-green eyes. Loyalty and helplessness. Marilyn suddenly wanted to please her – make her feel valued.

'I'm trying to remember the name, though . . .' she said. 'Gareth . . . Gareth who?'

Marilyn's life with Martin was so long ago it felt unreal. Its scenes and details became harder to discern through the passing years. But from time to time there was a distant afterglow or sudden stab of anger.

She might glimpse the two of them in a restaurant or spending a weekend with friends. Random things. She thought how young they must have looked.

Then the scenes of their break-up, when all that was familiar had suddenly and frighteningly disappeared.

There used to be a time when she toured the rooms of their old home in her imagination. They had also lived on a hill, in Bristol. Soft, blue-grey light in spring; the blossom of magnolias, alabaster-white in the dusk. She saw the pretty hand-printed wallpaper – pink roses drawn on an ivory background; elegant rugs and carefully chosen furniture. Panelling in the hallway stained sea-green.

Then she would imagine the same rooms emptied. The dark outlines left by pictures on the wall; the spaces where tables or sofas once stood. The afternoon light fading in the well-known rooms, as it always had.

But these thoughts were little more than details from snapshots, bordered by nothingness; and her interest in them was nearly gone – worn out over the years.

They had said everything, she and Martin. There was nothing left. The layers of time, though transparent, were too many now for her feelings to penetrate. These days, Marilyn lived in the present, for the most part, as she believed that any sensible person should. She had grown impatient with the past.

So she exercised every day, intensely. Running, yoga, weights. She knew all the best skincare products: day creams and night creams, serums and gels. She knew the rudiments of their science; loved their cold white perfumed world.

Her hair was arresting and stylish. Ash-blonde and silver – the colour was called Platinum Pearl – it fell to her broad shoulders in soft yet heavy locks.

Someone had said not long before that she looked as though she could throw off her clothes so easily.

Today she was wearing a black jersey, elegant and simple. The sleeves were pushed up to the elbow, revealing her brown forearms and a man's heavy gold sports watch, worn loosely around her left wrist like a bracelet. A length of fine gold chain glinted over her collar.

Her black tracksuit trousers were slightly baggy – made of some shiny, slippery-looking material that clung to her and showed off her legs when she moved.

The fabric was finely patterned in alternating diamonds of matt and lustrous black. Two long tags, each striped down its length with a band of rich leaf-green alongside another of bright scarlet, like military insignia, weighted at their ends with heavy gold clasps, hung lazily from the zip pockets.

Her feet were bare.

Just then, Marilyn turned to put down her drink. She stared into the drawing room and then turned away again.

She always seemed so calm and serious, her expression grave and gentle. The look in her dark eyes was as soft and warm as her mouth appeared to be. Her fine eyebrows were almost black beneath her silvery-blonde hair. And her forehead – her brow – was perfectly smooth. Men found her thrilling, for she carried the sadness of experience.

Meanwhile, Catherine was refilling her glass.

'Your parents look well.'

'Dad's been a little frail. I do worry about him.'

Bill and Josephine were standing side by side, receiving friends and well-wishers.

Serene yet faintly sinister in tinted glasses, Josephine still viewed the world as if from a more civilised dimension and with barely concealed amusement. Just when you thought she was really quite approachable she would put you back in your proper, lower, place with a question or comment so rude it threw you off balance.

To Catherine, for instance, that morning, she had said merely, 'Peaches and cream.'

But her half-dozen books on the history of Romantic music were respected.

She had come from money; and had the means, blonde and pretty in 1958, to toy with the young Bill Fuller until he didn't know which way was up. Tall and burly, his handsome head had been filled with Soviet cinema and the Cause.

Their world then was raucous parties in tall dilapidated houses. Kensington and Notting Hill. And their Gang had all been in the heroic phase of youth, as if no one had ever been young before them.

Josephine had watched it all, amused.

But one friend she had then, whom she almost treated as an equal. This was Basil: boyish and trim, so precise, snake-hipped. He wore grey silk shirts and Vaseline on his eyelashes. She called him 'Quint' and he called her 'Miss Jessel'. If he had an occupation, it seemed to be painting scenery for obscure plays.

Their favourite song was 'Red Hot Henry Brown' – a shiny old shellac record they had found in a box on the pavement, featuring 'comedienne with orchestra'.

'. . . he's Red Hot Henry Brown, the hottest man in town . . .'

Basil spoke fervently of Cocteau and Kim Novak – groaned when Josephine mentioned the Cause.

Josephine laughed and reported his derision to Bill.

But Basil was there at the birthday party, sixty years later, an honoured guest. Spry, impoverished, loving every minute.

Marilyn was not given to extravagant imaginings. But had she been, she might have pictured Josephine as being on loan from another world that was a silent library on a warm summer afternoon. There the smell of varnished shelves and old leather hung heavy. Windows looked out onto sunny lawns. Her clever mother, unblinking, stood by them in silence.

A second Josephine, meanwhile, her double, a serene and interested wanderer, had lived eight decades in London.

Marilyn glanced back into the corridor. The noise of conversation and laughter had grown louder. Chloe and her friend, still earnestly talking, kept eye contact so intensely. Catherine leant back against the kitchen worktop and drank her wine. Bill, in his heavy jumper, corduroy trousers and carpet slippers, looked tired but pleased. Josephine, straight-backed, was remote but polite.

Three

At midday Broadgate was cold and grey. So busy in summer, it reminded Martin now of a fallow field, slumbering through deepest winter. The surrounding City streets disappeared into pale mist. These first few days of February had been mean and unrelenting.

Through the railings to one side of the darkened wine bar you could see the platforms of Liverpool Street station spread out below.

Martin had stopped to look at the waterfall – the water green and freezing. His face wore a heavy, faraway look, remote and fixed like a blocking signal. Watching the miniature cascade he felt the weight and depth of spent time.

'*It is the ease and frequency with which you lie to me.*'

So began Marilyn's last letter to him. The words were engraved on his life. He had found her note nearly fifteen years earlier in the inside pocket of his jacket. The sheet of writing paper was sharply folded in a narrow envelope made of thick cream-coloured paper, sealed tightly shut. His name was written on it in black ink, in neat, firm, swift characters.

He had been amid the crowds on Victoria station, waiting to catch a train to his mother's suburb. A cold spring evening of torrential rain. Such were the final minutes of the life he had known with Marilyn, that had defined them both for almost twenty years.

Absurdly, Martin had been struck by the elegance of her prose. Marilyn was of a higher social class, of course, to himself – metropolitan intelligentsia who stood on their inherited money as on islands. But he had been shocked to notice, at this moment of catastrophe, that their separation assaulted his sense of status.

He longed to hold her and beg for everything to be how it had been years earlier; was then aware of his heavy bag and wet coat. His ageing mother's worries and needs to be attended to – when everything was now chaotic. He was filled with panic.

But he sat on the train and saw the familiar suburbs pass by. It had stopped raining. The dusk sky was clearing to pink and pale blue; the stars were a lightly thrown handful of small diamonds.

Marilyn had loved him so much. A terrifying chasm had opened before him. He stared at the gathering evening, stilled by grief and shock, unthinking. Everything beautiful, for him, came back to Marilyn.

Now, in the misty City, fifteen years later, Martin felt both the silence within himself and the rip tide of the past. These days he often had moments when he just wanted to apologise to everyone he had ever known for everything he had ever done.

There was the small lift, its back wall a mirror, to one side of the unattended and overheated hallway in Caulfield House.

Three of the five floors were locked off. Martin got out on the second floor, as he did each week. Three big sealed windows admitted a kind of twilight to the small waiting area and short corridor that led to Colin's office.

His overcoat and scarf beside him, Martin sat on the low sofa and stared at the windows that were filled with grey sky.

Luke Barnes at the office had once confided – his expression earnest and resentful – that when *he* had gone to therapy, a few years back, near London Bridge station – Tooley Street – he had been asked by the therapist, before they even began, to sign a contract agreeing not to commit suicide.

'And it goes on your record' – he had gravely concluded his tale.

Every office had one of Luke's kind. Angry, with-drawn, fearful, needy.

Martin had worked in so many offices over the years.

The first had been in Croydon, when he was just nineteen: a holiday job not far from the shopping centre. The office towers with their space-age names – Zodiac House, Lunar House . . . The cool subway into blinding sun; strange hot weeks, trying not to think about the way that Francesca – his first girlfriend – had dropped him so brutally.

When the crisis came, 'It just goes in one ear and out the other,' she had exclaimed, finally, indurate to his tearful entreaties. Her tone was cold, long-suffering. That of a busy official pestered to the limits of their patience. Practicality, clearly, was the assassin dispatched by women to murder romance.

After Francesca, the offices began. It was like seeing a warm concrete world through glass.

What next? Monument, Baker Street, Blackfriars, Ludgate Circus – there, two buildings, the same firm. Even the lobbies barely changed; nor the lifts, nor the old stairwells that smelt of warm dust and cardboard.

And the figures met along the stages of office life's way, over the years. Robert Groom, for instance, so many offices ago.

Toweringly huge with greying curly hair and a fat face, his small silver-blue eyes had promised lunatic humour. He wore an ageless evergreen corduroy suit. And that scything upper-class voice; pronouncing 'Brian', for example – as in their line manager, Brian Shepherd – 'Brarn'.

Robert had been a grand bohemian who temped; then disappeared for weeks on end – house-sitting in Barons Court for an Austrian count, he said. The count was a Buddhist.

Robert had told Martin the story of how, now that he was poor – 'I have forsaken worldly possessions', the words rolled out in a nasal drawl — he had stayed in dozens of different houses and flats in London, 'West and Central', over the years. Then one cold night he had come out of the French restaurant he frequented on Charlotte Street and — '*Shit*. I've forgotten where I live.'

He had said it briskly, squeakily, with a frown — addressing, irritated, the vagaries of a pettily hostile universe, as though someone had pinched his raincoat.

Martin had never forgotten the tale.

'Hi, Martin — come on in.'

He heard Colin's quiet unaccented voice; and there he was, looking down at his client. He was a man of medium build with sandy hair and a narrow, rather pinched face. He wore glasses with very thin metal frames. He was dressed casually, in a brown pullover and cream-coloured jeans. His clients usually managed to avoid one another, as Martin had heard ghosts do.

Martin rose to his feet, gathered up his coat and scarf.

The office door was ajar. The white room was filled with bright light. It reminded Martin of the light off morning snow. They took their seats in armchairs.

'So, how's it been going?' — Colin was flicking back through his notes. 'You were saying last time about nightmares?'

He looked up at Martin, unblinking. His narrow face was expressionless yet expectant.

'I don't know whether I'd call them nightmares,' said Martin.

He was aware of his own voice. It sounded slightly muffled.

33

'Yes?'

'There were four. They were on consecutive nights, I think. It was more that they were extremely vivid . . .'

Colin's expression was unchanged but he gave a very small nod.

Martin felt uncertain. It seemed ridiculous, recounting his dreams.

'Dreams fall apart when you put them into words.'

'But they can sometimes tell us whether we're anxious or angry, or . . .'

'Yes?'

'Yes. I think it's possible.'

The previous week, Colin had asked Martin about his schooldays.

Martin had tried to remember. In his mind's eye he saw autumnal scenes: playing fields, old classrooms, a few unwelcome faces. But he had wanted to remember and describe his experience precisely.

It was vague in places, all too vivid in others.

'At my first school I think I was happy,' he said at last. 'At the second – I was sad, ashamed, afraid. A failure.'

Colin's expression was suddenly understanding.

'Good at beating yourself up, aren't you?'

But to Martin it had felt like they were just chatting, which he found unbearable. The minutes ticked by.

'Are you still drinking a lot?' Colin was saying.

'On and off.'

'How many days have you missed work? In the last month?'

Martin couldn't remember. It hadn't been so bad. 'A few.'

There was a flare of doubt in Colin's eyes, but all he did was nod.

'What else?' he asked.

Martin looked towards the window. Seeing the low grey clouds, he longed for the elevated tracks and the fresher air, higher up. He glanced up for a second, then made a gesture as if to say, 'There's nothing else.'

'How are you fixed for next week?' Colin was looking in his diary, suddenly speaking in a totally different tone of voice.

A little under ninety minutes later Martin was standing halfway down the platform at Moorgate station. He had gone back to the office in the meantime, but done nothing.

Tim Hallett had leant over his desk and made a necromantic pass in the air with one hand. 'It's all a dream!' he proclaimed, in an urgent breathless voice, and then walked off, laughing.

Martin had smiled – as you might give an irritating child a tired smile; then turned back to his screen and the smile dropped away immediately.

The Tube train, brightly lit, half empty, clattered in. Taking his seat Martin watched the platform advertisements flicking by, becoming a blur. Then he remembered a record that began with a young woman's voice – sulky-tough-bored – intoning the songs title: 'I am a cliché . . .'

Then an echoing beat of silence before her motor-mouth vocal, high-speed fretsaw guitar and drums; haphazard surfer-rock, a toddler tantrum in Morse code . . . The same phrase, over and over. She couldn't actually repeat the words fast enough.

She had died young.

These days, Martin's half-formed thoughts meandered, it was difficult to know whether it was hot or cold; it was both. And two days in London could seem like a year, and a year like a day and a half. Days could be dark but humid, first oppressive then suddenly chill, like the cold sweat before a faint.

The young man next to him was reading an old paperback book called *The Moon of Chronic Stress*.

This brought Hannah Wye to mind. Esoteric publishing. He had known Hannah for nearly thirty years. She had been a friend to both him and Marilyn – together, separately – yet never easy to get to know.

Tall – 'impressive' had been Marilyn's description – her long brown hair was streaked red–gold and fell in loosely stretched ringlets between her shoulder blades. She wore an oily dark-crimson lipstick. Her reading glasses were antique tortoiseshell.

When she was younger Hannah had created what she called her 'spinster librarian' look: kilt pins, sensible shoes, brown stockings, tight sweater; had in fact been a minor celebrity – model, face – in the final gloaming of the style press years, early nineties. The cool Soho eccentric. She was after all a genuine Londoner.

In those days she wore violet face powder and her hair was dyed the colour of vanilla ice cream. The roots showed through, the colour of dried mud. She was archaically busty; had long legs, heather-flecked tweeds, a face like a Spanish painting. Someone said she was the first woman in London to speak like a bitchy gay man – before it was the norm; as if she were constantly gathering material for an acerbic memoir.

She worked in Lamb's Conduit Street and had done for as long as Martin could remember – since '87, '88 . . . – book design, or a design agency, perhaps . . . She was self-educated, literary, keen on local history; from one of the old Crown Estates – Regent's Park by Camden Town. Children playing in an echoing courtyard; a world of women and old photographs of shyly cheerful relatives.

She was much quieter these days and more serious.

'Your trouble,' she had once told Martin, 'is that for you, atmosphere always atrophies action.'

'Sorry?'

The previous September, late summer 2016, Hannah and Martin had met for coffee at a corner café not far from Theobalds Road. It was still warm enough to sit outside so Hannah could smoke.

'Maybe you get what you wish for,' she had said. She turned to face Martin. 'And then you get into the habit of undoing the habit of having.'

Martin looked blank and said nothing.

'Suppose you'd been given it all,' she went on, 'or the means to have it. Everything that would have made

37

you content. And then you managed to systematically undo it all without even really knowing why. Fuck it all up completely. Laziness, stupidity – wanting more pleasure.'

'What can I say?' Martin couldn't tell whether or not she was being serious.

'I was in Selfridges the other day; that new champagne bar they have with all the mirrors. A hundred different champagnes or something. Then you think of our parents' generation – what they had. Crazy.'

Martin studied her profile: the shadow of her jaw, her painted lips parting slightly as she raised a cigarette to her mouth. She stared ahead for a moment, her brown-green eyes barely blinking.

Then he said, 'Since I was fifteen I've spent my life reading books either by or about dead homosexuals. And now my conversation is comprised solely of reminiscences. Every fifty paces I stop to look for something that's gone. Some shitty pub where I once saw The Damned. That kind of thing.'

'That's like having sex to feel young again,' Hannah replied. 'I once went to bed with someone solely because I thought it would bring back the feeling of being at school.'

'Really? Did it?'

She didn't answer; and so they sat for a while longer in the sunshine, stilled by its mood.

Then Martin could feel the weight of being himself – the heavy black bag, awkward and tiring, that he had been carrying around for as long as he could remember.

Lugging it up the escalator; and now he could barely walk – the flame-hot iron shoes . . .

'I *am* a cliché,' he said, flatly.

'You know what Chloe said?' Hannah turned once more to face him. 'That when you talk about punk you sound like your mother talking about the war – "What did *you* do in the Punk War, Daddy?"'

Chloe Ann Fuller – she had taken Marilyn's family name on her eighteenth birthday. Their only child. Born at home in Bristol in early January '91 – as first snow was falling on the prosperous communal garden. In a gone world he had watched the big flakes settle on the old beech hedge, the sandstone sundial barely visible in the middle of the lawn.

Then he was back on the Tube train, the doors sliding open at Farringdon station, in the middle of the busy working day. Another day, another lunch. He had to be back at the office for a meeting at 3.30 p.m.

As he left the station he felt the damp fresh air on his face and a few spots of rain.

Gareth, Gareth, Gareth . . .

In their own ways, Marilyn, Martin and Catherine had all given thought to that name and its owner, over the years.

Martin, on the face of it, was the most qualified to have an opinion. He had indeed known Gareth quite well, at college in Liverpool. They met in late November 1978.

39

These days, his time in Liverpool seemed little more than a dream. Had it even happened?

But as he found it then, the college library was a new addition built of concrete. The air inside felt hot and heavy. Martin had imagined becoming a denizen of the place – the Romantic scholar. So there he sat on the fourth floor of that building, for perhaps a morning and three afternoons in all, surrounded by impressive-looking tomes.

What might interest him?

He had called up a two-volume study of Goethe. When the books were delivered they turned out to be written in German. He spent twenty minutes in awe of their intricate Gothic typeface. Then he collected his bag and went downstairs to the coffee bar.

The dozen or so tables were always crowded, littered with dirty polystyrene cups, overflowing ashtrays and biscuit wrappers. People sat on the floor too; leaning against the wall or huddled in groups.

Martin, friendless, had already studied the mass of his contemporaries. Taken soundings of the crowd.

Neither long hair nor short was most in evidence, on students of either sex; rather, there was a formless sameness of shape and shade – heavy, dull, unkempt. It set the mood. Against the northern rain and chill were jeans and thick pullovers, drab jackets, long heavy coats and broad woollen scarves.

Martin found a place at a table by the wall and lit a cigarette. He was wearing black nail polish and was unutterably bored and frustrated. All he wanted to do was leave; get on a train back to London and be with Francesca, then still his girlfriend.

It was she who had given him the nail polish; and it was her scent – Opium – that he could smell on the navy silk pocket square that he always kept with him.

But that particular afternoon even the thought of Francesca was queasy with unease. For Martin felt sure he had noticed a cooling of her need for him; a need in which he had luxuriated, blissful and serene, as if in an amniotic sac of pure pleasure. Was there now, he wondered, an edge – or worse, a flatness – in her voice when he called her, which was most evenings?

He gnawed at the thought as it gnawed at him. He knew the location of every payphone; even a brace of dank dark booths in the shadow of the multistorey car park.

During the afternoon, however, he did not dare call. And surely even that – when once she had sounded so thrilled, so brimming with excited adoration, simply to hear his voice – was confirmation of his worries?

He sipped his pallid coffee and lit another cigarette. He felt adrift, nervous. He looked again at his fellow students.

All were strangers to him. None elicited his interest. There were sallow young men with shoulder-length hair and lightly bearded chins that rested on the high rolled necks of their jumpers. Others had pale childlike faces, and wore heavily framed glasses. Then there was a scattering of male athletes, rowers and rugby players, with broad grins and big chins, who held their cups of coffee like a race of giants obliged to use human crockery.

The female students likewise congregated in a vast uniformity of denim, brown wool, thick hair and black coats. They had between them clear complexions, centre partings, hair grips, red hands, earmuffs, shy expressions, snub noses, shoulder bags made of sacking, and thick files spilling dog-eared papers. Some were pretty, some plain; some dour, others smiling. One blew her nose, another laughed as she rummaged in her bag; a third sat with her chin resting on her neighbour's shoulder, not blinking.

But the very sight of them all, so at ease, so seemingly lacking urgency of any kind, made the aesthete tap his right foot very fast against the metal table leg. A common spirit held them all together, reasonably content, at ease in their situation.

Many of them, he was sure, were far cleverer than he would ever be; had knowledge and ideas that they saw no need to wear like a badge. But he had dismissed them all, solely and instantly on the basis of their appearance and demeanour.

Martin felt sure his impatience would soon draw unwanted attention. Then they would see him – and be utterly indifferent, at most amused. And that's where Goethe and Francesca had got him. There and to the void, blank yet tense, that his life seemed to have revealed itself to be.

Very rarely, an individual would appear in the crowded coffee bar who was clearly of a different sort.

There had been an olive-skinned young man with neatly cut and brilliantined black hair, for instance, who wore a white shirt, narrow claret silk tie, grey flannel trousers and a jacket of moss-green-coloured light tweed. He sported a Clark Gable moustache and was smoking French cigarettes. With him was an auburn-haired girl with pale skin and grey eyes, dressed entirely in black, who sat very erect as she applied her scarlet lipstick, a thin diamanté bracelet slipping down her white forearm.

Where these exotic creatures came from and went, Martin had no idea. He had noticed that the man's accent was that of Merseyside. They had the air of people simply passing through; of being from the centre of what was most fashionable and most exclusive – but what? He imagined a club – a kind of Palm Court winter garden, part Paris 1919, part rockabilly, with café tables and damson drapes.

But it was as though such characters were invisible to the rest of the students. They carried on their conversations, laughter and exclamations with their heads turned casually away from these emissaries of another surely more enlightened world, whom Martin found so arresting.

Comparing the aloof red-lipstick girl with Francesca, however – whose hair was also auburn – Martin was attracted to the stranger's theatricality even as he found her features rather coarse. He thought again of the gentle alluring warmth, the softly golden youthfulness – as he found it – of his London suburban beloved.

Having nothing else to do and being incapable of action, Martin stayed on in the coffee bar. His inertia raised him up, like an aircraft ascending through the ceiling of cloud, to a place that seemed calmer and quieter; and from where, stilled, he could look down at the world below. The afternoon rush had died down. He bought another coffee and went back to his table . . .

He became aware of Gareth's presence before he actually saw him. Later, he would think it was as though the air had actually quickened or tensed – some atmospheric shift as if time itself had suddenly stood to attention.

Martin had just raised his cigarette to his lips. He noticed that his nail polish had chipped and there was a rust-yellow nicotine stain between his fingers. Then there was the sense of someone approaching, as if at speed.

Unlike most of the students, Gareth neither ambled nor strolled nor marched with businesslike purpose. Rather, he strode – determined and military, as if between two far more exciting places. His imminent arrival commanded his surroundings. And he strode past Martin that afternoon as though he, too, didn't need to look at him to see him.

The lone aesthete's first impression of Gareth was of someone from a film. A character who was neither good nor bad – ambiguous rather, aware of the fact and inclined to make use of it. Physically, Gareth dominated, tall and broad-chested.

The first time he turned and looked directly at Martin his stare was insolently superior. He had black hair that was cut very short at the sides, loosely curling on top. His face was pale and his eyes blue. His mouth – onlookers might say – was cruel.

He was dressed that weekday afternoon in scarlet parachute trousers that tapered at the ankle, black Chelsea boots with leather soles and an old and faded black t-shirt. A black leather jacket, antique and glorious, hung loosely off his shoulders. Slipped into the neck of his t-shirt was a pair of sunglasses, the frames and lenses very black.

The effect of this impressive ensemble was not wasted on Martin; and was thrown into wholly new territory by the inverted bright-fuchsia-pink triangle that he then saw was dyed into Gareth's hair at the back.

This was also the colour, he recognised, of the silk blouse that Francesca wore with her white denim skirt.

Gareth meanwhile had stopped. He turned again, very deliberately, and stared at Martin for a moment; then, raising his eyebrows and twisting the corner of his mouth, shook his head with a sardonic expression of weary disappointment.

Around the table in the meeting room were Richard, Emil, Tim Hallett, Sofia, Luke Barnes and Martin.

This was a bad time for Martin – mid-afternoon; he felt so decrepit, awake but asleep, his eyelids mercilessly heavy.

The others were talking about a building project – something to do with tax. Their discussion was complex, energetic and technical.

When each spoke, a certain expression came into their eyes – a sudden vigilance; as though, Martin imagined, hostage within the eternal winter landscape of a post-apocalyptic city, they each had to take their watch above ground, scanning the endless blast-bleached rubble; even as a few stray snowflakes fell from the dusk sky, blew against the warm cheek or caught on an eyelash; to be brushed away unthinkingly as they peered, looking as hard as it was possible to look, into a gathering darkness that might know whether or not they would see out the night.

Watching the suddenly online eyes of his colleagues engage across the table, Martin glanced up at the low ceiling with its curiously textured panels like photographs of the lunar surface. This was the way modern adults engaged with the world, he thought. Not the punk war, nor the pink triangle, the lunar surface.

'. . . if the accounting period straddles the commencement date . . .' Emil was saying.

'—on a reasonable basis, factoring a compensation payment . . .' – that was Sofia.

They spoke as though Martin was not there. He cleared his throat, just lightly – experimentally.

'. . . I'd have to check, but in the case of non-registered . . .'

'—to accept their summary update.'

46

No one had noticed his cough, so Martin thought again of Robert Groom. Leaving the restaurant on Charlotte Street – Elena's L'Etoile, so long ago – unable to remember where he lived. Standing there by the kerb in the icy cold, swaying slightly, serious-faced, his mind suddenly blank, the Rolodex spinning.

And here I am, Martin reasoned, and I don't really know what my job is any more. He surely felt how Robert must have felt, only permanently. As for his 'skill' – it had been known as so many things over the years; been in and out of fashion, regarded as both Saviour and Antichrist: logistics, IT, data management, tech, systems analyst . . . Now it was everything and nothing, like most things.

Then Martin remembered other silences. Had his family ever asked him anything about himself, genuinely interested? Not especially. But had he ever wanted them to?

The silence of school, of the concrete library, of the office; as though he was there but not there. Marilyn was another silence, now. When he tried to speak with her – which was nearly always on the phone – he could not find words or form sentences. He mumbled, when he had never mumbled.

Perhaps the pursuit of the interesting made you invisible.

Four

'You're magnetised,' Hannah said to Martin at lunch.

It was Thursday, 9 February 2017 and sudden freezing weather.

Martin lifted his chin, raised his eyebrows and stared at her, not blinking.

'Very born-to-rule,' said Hannah.

'Meaning?'

'Your expression, now.'

'No, I meant – what do you mean, "magnetised"?'

Hannah wiped the rim of her wine glass with her thumb. 'I think people are thinking about you.'

Martin felt flattered and anxious – noticing as he did so that he knew this uneasy mix of feelings quite well.

'Ah! Mysterious,' she added.

'I wish I knew what you meant,' he said. 'But it sounds reasonably—'

'Maybe your spirit ancestors are gathering at the foot of your bed.'

'Oh. Great.'

'That's not necessarily a bad thing. Why do you automatically think it's a bad thing?'

Martin wanted to get away from the subject.

'I heard from Marilyn,' he said. 'I think there was slightly less frost – just slightly. Maybe I imagined it.'

'Did she ask if you were seeing anyone?'

'No . . . No . . .' Martin sounded suddenly uncertain. 'Why? Is she?'

'Are you asking me? I don't know.' Hannah widened her green eyes. 'I'd love another drink.'

'I can't believe I didn't know about this place.' Martin glanced around the small room. 'It's really nice . . . I can't think anyone's going to miss me . . .'

Soon two more glasses of the heady house red wine stood before them. All was well and manageable. A cosy dark London day in a nice little restaurant.

Hannah had gone outside to smoke a cigarette, despite the cold. Martin turned in his chair and leant against dark panelling. Suddenly it felt rather appropriate – becoming – to be magnetised.

The previous evening he had had dinner with Chloe and her friend Alice. They made a striking couple. But intentionally? He had almost mentioned it to Marilyn that morning, but their talk had been going quite well . . . The slightest disturbance . . .

'Everything good?' Hannah resumed her seat.

'Just thinking – sitting and thinking.'

'Of what were you thinking?'

'My spirit ancestors, mostly.'

★

Then it was shortly after six fifteen in the evening.

After seeing Hannah and being unable to decide what to do, Martin had gone back to the office. He still felt slightly high from the wine at lunch.

Nearly everyone had gone home. A moment came when the office fell quiet; as though the low persistent drone of an engine that had been running all day had suddenly stopped. One or two background noises sounded louder. Some voices down the corridor – a man and a woman. Then the abrupt metallic spooling and rhythmic rustling clicks of a document being printed.

At his desk beside the floor-to-ceiling windows of the sixth floor – the only perk that age had brought him – Martin had a view diagonally north up Bishopsgate.

He always stayed at the office until nearly seven. This had assured his reputation as a reliable old hand. Once or twice, quite early on, he had been noticed by those above him and those below him in the office hierarchy, sitting there long after six, peering at his screen, jabbing away at his keyboard – and all with an entirely accidental expression of utmost seriousness.

After that, nobody had questioned him or maybe even noticed him ever again.

Just before dusk, the busy street below filled with silvery light. There were a few grey clouds over Spitalfields – home of Martin and Marilyn's old friends Julian and Paul, now married.

Years ago, back in Bristol, the long weekends when those two came to stay had always been the happiest and most fun. Long meals, old films, late breakfasts. Marilyn adored Julian and Paul.

When Martin surveyed his generation, these two men were the only couple he could think of who had stayed together.

'Although I think they have an arrangement . . .' he had mentioned to Stuart during the gin and tonic overture to one of their fish suppers.

In the quiet office, Martin frowned. That must have been at least two years ago, maybe three – but he remembered the evening quite clearly.

Off the back of a second large gin they had started to laugh.

'Ah, well—'

'Absolutely!'

'. . . with a woman. I mean, "See you later, darling – I'm just off to that orgy . . ." Can you imagine?'

'Actually, did I ever tell you about Liz? It seems that Stefan—'

Then, a little later, earnest and effusive as the alcohol hit mid-tempo:

'The thing is, you've met them; they're so great and they do have an amazing relationship. They met at college in Brighton – it must have been the early eighties. All peaked caps and every-night-is-Friday-night; drag queens dressed as Stevie Nicks, that kind of thing. And then Julian made a *lot* of money in advertising . . .'

'Funny how you never really hear of people working in advertising these days. It used to be all the rage.'

'Then they bought that enormous house in East Dulwich . . .'

'Oh, I'd forgotten that . . .'

'. . . and now they've got the house in Spitalfields – Georgian, huge; and it hasn't been fiddled around with – the whole thing . . . what? Four, five floors in all?'

'And Paul doesn't mind Julian being . . . adventurous?'

'I gather not.'

Stuart drank fast, seemingly with little effect – until later, attempting to stand. Then how charming and clever and funny they had found their inebriation. Outside in the sudden cold, close by London Bridge; the last trains rattling overhead towards New Cross, Blackheath, Lewisham . . .

On the pavement the two men faced one another, swaying a little, barely able to speak. Then they had gone their separate ways.

Almost immediately, staggering slightly, Martin had felt drear darkness gather in his thoughts. The hangover waiting; the pointless self-hate. How many days lost that month? The world was no longer splendid and entertaining and he a witty and stylish commentator upon it. He was the kind of person he had watched from cabs, late at night, trapped in the dark tunnel of their lives; walking hunched and falling forward every few steps.

On his way home he had bought a bottle of gin at the local twenty-four-hour store, City News. There had

been something about the shop owner's expression . . .
That small but noticeable mix of surprise and slight disgust – of decency affronted. The friend by the hearth . . .

Martin looked again towards Spitalfields, taking his bearings from the white spire of Christ Church.

Then he remembered how Paul, the one-time monkey-faced elfin boy, shaved head and Harrington jacket, Joni Mitchell beret, had opened the glossy coal-black front door to the house on Princelet Street – what? Ten, twelve years ago?

Such a broad smile. The sage-green panelling and the smell of money like the smell of a funeral parlour – lilies, stone and cold water. Overhead the palest sky-blue ceiling.

'It's how it would have been when it was new . . .' Paul had said, leading the way up sharply creaking stairs to a landing and sash window filled with the same silvery winter light. 'We'd like to use candles but it's a timber-framed street . . .'

Then Julian had appeared. He was only slightly older than Paul but looked much older, tall and broad in his immaculate evergreen pullover and grey flannel trousers. Blonde, his thinning hair swept back off his high academic-looking forehead. Cheekbones like wing mirrors.

Martin had remembered that the couple also owned a house in Arles with a fragrant garden: sun-bleached wooden chairs with pretty Moroccan cushions; dusty terracotta pots, pink and white geraniums; a jasmine trellis, scurrying lizards . . . Marilyn was a regular visitor, in her crisp and blousy cream cotton dress and big dark glasses; simple summer sandals that cost a fortune . . .

At Princelet Street that winter afternoon, coming on for dusk, he had sat with the two men in their first-floor sitting room. The principal rooms downstairs had been turned into a library and dining room respectively, reached by tall tobacco-brown doors that opened off either side of the chilly, dim-lit hall – an antique longcase clock gravely ticking in the dust-coloured half-light.

Down a short dark corridor could be found the sunny kitchen; big enough for weekend breakfast parties at the long Victorian refectory table. Also for the caterers and hired butler (biracial, chic; her services – her presence even, her aura – in constant demand from Shoreditch to Shepherd's Bush) when Julian and Paul entertained more seriously . . .

In the upstairs sitting room, overlooking the narrow street, three more sash windows admitted a surprising amount of light, their big wooden shutters folded back onto themselves.

Facing into the room were two narrow armchairs of Arts and Crafts design, the embroidered upholstery poetically well worn. To one side, opposite the white marble fireplace, an English Regency sofa with cushions a pale-pink blush, fringed with gold. Against the far wall stood an upright piano, lid open; an antique Bechstein, ebony-black. Beneath a valuable threadbare rug, the broad, highly polished floorboards dipped down to one side.

'The gentleman who used to live here,' said Julian, slowly, with relish – all the time in the world to tell his anecdote – 'explained that if you dropped a collar stud in this room you would always know where to find it, because it could only roll in one direction. But a collar stud, imagine!'

Paul, leaning forward over the back of a rosewood chair, gently rocking himself to and fro, had grinned encouragingly at their guest. The couple had reached a place in prosperous middle age, Martin saw, where life was one big lark – there for pleasure, to be found amusing and delightful.

The panelling, intact and uneven, with hair-line splits running vertically here and there – '. . . because the whole building is actually moving,' Julian explained, 'like it's alive' – was likewise painted pale sage-green.

'And seriously illegal,' Paul chipped in. 'Julian researched it. He had some flakes of the original paint tested, from, like, 1726 . . . And then we met this lovely man who works for the National Front or whatever—'

'National Trust!' Julian corrected him, with theatrical exasperation.

'—or whatever,' Paul continued defiantly, 'and he had it made up for us on the quiet by some company out in Essex. They do a roaring trade. It's jam-packed with lead and hair and horse-bone glue and God knows what. Flouts every building regulation known to man. But hey, it looks pretty.'

Martin had studied the two men, who were so at ease. He was the lumbering heterosexual, bringing his grubby news.

'The fireplace is Grade I listed, funnily enough, while the rest of the house is Grade II . . .' Julian was explaining. 'We never quite found out why.'

Again, life and circumstances had presented the comfortable couple with a delightful, flattering little mystery to be shared with amused bemusement.

Had he and Marilyn been like that, Martin had wondered, when visitors stayed at their home? He feared that he, at least, had been far worse. The duke in his domain. Marilyn would be incapable of such behaviour, of even conceiving of it . . .

He'd glanced up at a large brownish painting set in a thick black wooden frame. It depicted an overcast city street, down which a jumble of blustery autumn weather-battered citizens processed. One, a gentleman, startlingly lavender-faced and red-moustachioed, with small, dot-like, pitch-black eyes and a grey bowler hat tilted jauntily to one side, stared out into the room, quizzically, eerily, into the real-world silence; while the red-haired woman beside him looked down, busy in their afternoon world. Then other passers-by in near silhouette, hurrying along an avenue or boulevard – a blur of high grey buildings; then more browns and dank rust-orange and murky black conifer-greens . . .

Austrian . . . Early twentieth century – significant; a wedding present from Julian's friend, an older man, Oliver.

Martin sat in one of the armchairs. There was a small circular table between him and Julian. He held a generous gin and tonic in his lap very carefully.

'You may already have heard . . .' he began, apologetically, he noticed. Julian sat with his hands on his knees, expressionless. Paul had suddenly stood up very straight, his hands in his pockets, but was still smiling. Was his smile slightly knowing? An ill-concealed smirk?

'. . . about Marilyn and I . . .'

A sudden exhalation. 'We're both so sorry,' said Julian.

'It's – the end of an era!' said Paul.

'Well, I don't want to try to massage the facts. It's a mess and I wanted to let you know myself.'

'How's Chloe taking it?'

Julian, thought Martin, sounded rather blasé. And the question was surely premature? He had barely begun his version of events, only to be instantly cut off, as if this was of no consequence. Julian and Paul were Chloe's godparents, but . . . he felt his face becoming hot.

Julian and Paul lived in a world where nobody had anything as non-negotiable and messily immediate as children. 'None of our friends have children. Even our friends' *dogs* don't have children,' Julian had once said – much to Martin and Marilyn's cosy fireside amusement.

'When your niece came to stay,' Paul had reminded his partner on that occasion, 'and she was sick in our bed, remember? It was just, like, *everything* had to stop . . .'

58

Nodding, Julian had given the mirthless smile of one forced to deal with an unjust and impossible situation.

Martin thought of Chloe – several memories of her, all at once. Back then, a child in the terrible aftermath; the previous evening, a poised young woman. She had Marilyn's accent, only more forceful – louder. Very clear intonation; she contained not a trace of suburbia – of his side of the family.

She had once trusted him completely and loved him unconditionally. Now she came in and out of focus, sometimes close, sometimes distant.

Back in Princelet Street, he had said to her godparents, vaguely and less than persuasively, 'She's fine; she'll be fine . . .'

Then Paul had darted across the room. 'A little visit from the god of gin. Do you need more tonic?'

Those words, in particular, had stayed with him. For, suddenly exhausted, Martin – the handsome fragile alien – had leant back and taken a deep drink, then another. He drank as though he was on his own and very thirsty and the glass was filled with water. He closed his eyes, his head tipped back, not caring what impression he made. It wasn't planned; it just happened. Then he held his glass up for a refill – his wish immediately granted.

He had stared at the ceiling for a moment, beginning to feel pleasantly detached – surrounded this time by a silence more watchful than tactful. All was lost, he thought. This is either my fate or my choice. It was like simply and easily falling backwards.

Drunkenly he cast his net upon welcoming chaos. He could start with science fiction. He would never get back to his own solar system, not now; never prove his species, his race, his mission and his need. But who cared? He had enough money; could always find ways to stay high, women . . .

'I think we've been apart for some years,' he had said, flatly, his voice a little thickened. 'But with my work – in London mostly; then coming home late on Friday nights, exhausted . . .'

. . . Falling asleep on the last train and waking up dry-mouthed and surly in a deserted carriage; staring depressed at the empty wine bottles and abandoned newspapers . . .

'There was just nothing left that brought us together. We'd had separate rooms for years; we'd stopped going anywhere; we didn't even eat together or watch a film together. Marilyn was always busy, whatever that meant; on some new diet or yoga thing; and always making sure that Chloe was busy or exhausted – one or the other. I felt they just didn't want me in the house; that I spoilt their mother-and-daughter world. It was a horrible feeling – to be inched out, room by room.'

He was aware that he sounded aggressive – worse, peevish; also that his voice now sounded muffled and far away; first sign, or one of them, of drunkenness. But he ploughed on, his speech accelerating. 'When we tried to discuss it, Marilyn always said that she wanted us to stay together – but she never looked remotely happy at the prospect. So on Saturday nights I used to go for dinner by myself at that Browns place at the bottom of the hill – do you remember it? We all went there once. And that was the beginning of the end, really . . . Or the middle of the end – Browns . . .'

Julian still looked down, his mouth set in a straight line, nodding very slightly. Then he looked up, across at Martin, and opened his hands in a gesture of helplessness. Sad smile. Paul meanwhile had wandered over to the piano and was standing sideways to it, resting one knee on the cushion of the rickety Victorian piano stool. A few staccato chords, soft but emphatic, filled the room. Was he bored already?

Julian's expression was hard to read. He suddenly seemed different – no longer an old and understanding friend in whom one could confide, completely and without judgement.

Paul's chords meanwhile had become a little louder, steadily paced; then descended a couple of octaves with a suave abbreviated arpeggio, to carry them into a minor key . . .

'*Hey kids, shake it loose together,*' he half-sang to himself.

'Paul!' Julian turned to his partner, widening his eyes in a pointed manner. 'Time and place, no?'

Resigned and confused, Martin thought only of gin. He had caught the slight, knowing smile – there for barely a second – as Julian reprimanded his partner. His news after all was the only ugly thing in their beautiful house.

'I think Marilyn just wants to be angry,' he heard himself saying. 'Which is probably easier for her than having to accept that she isn't entirely blameless in this . . .'

'Well . . .'

Julian knew – because Marilyn had told him – that Martin had gone to bed with a woman in London; some old girlfriend? He couldn't remember the details because they had been of no great interest to him.

Then Martin had been drunk and in the remorse of a two-day hangover had tried to tell Marilyn about it.

'Which might have made him feel better,' Julian had said to Paul at the time, 'but what was she supposed to do with the news? Honestly . . .'

Paul had said nothing to this. He chose to look blank and then hummed a little tune.

The long weekends of late breakfasts and old films were far away.

Marilyn had been seated, silent, her hands in her lap. During Martin's rambling account of his actions it seemed as though the man she knew, had known for years, had never existed.

She looked down, unable for some reason to feel her hands. Her breath came in quick gasps. Martin had never seen her like that before. He kept repeating how sorry he was.

Suddenly standing, she had blazed at him, her eyes flashing and terrible.

'Why are you sorry?' Her tone was savage but her voice was very clear and level. 'You keep saying you're sorry. It's very annoying. I don't get it. What are you so sorry about?'

Martin had tried to hold her. For a second or two she was in his arms, but rigid. The fine soft wool of her cardigan was warm. Perhaps it would all be—

'I can't feel anything.' The words were cold and hard. She shoved him away – a violent push in his ribs.

Then she left the room. The following morning she and Chloe were gone, driving to her parents' house. He heard nothing more from her until he found her letter, there amid the rain-soaked crowds on Victoria station.

It was as though he had sent himself back in time – back to his beginning; only now the beginning was already dirtied and stale and used up. There could be no redress, however he told the tale.

Then, for years, nothing ever got better.

The sixth floor returned and the City night through vast office windows. Martin sat back in his black mesh chair and felt very still. He slowly closed his eyes.

He remembered the dusk light in the upstairs room at Princelet Street – the silvery London light; and how, buoyed on yet another gin, he had managed to make it back into the facile, heroic phase of drunkenness – getting on the roller coaster . . . The glorious gale . . . He and Paul and Julian had gone for dinner somewhere smart; and for a few hours all had been at ease and for the best.

Alone in the office, Martin felt too tired to compete any more that day in the game of life.

It was getting on for seven thirty in the evening. He stood up, his legs and back feeling stiff, and reached for his jacket. He felt tired, heavily so; an odd feeling that he couldn't quite place, like he was coming down with something.

He looked at the street and traffic far below; the black cabs pushing south with their lights on, the hunched cyclists racing north. All was silenced, from where he stood.

Five

Marilyn, five miles to the west, was at that moment parking her car in a side street in Marylebone.

Her fondness for new, fast cars was either a quirk or – as Martin had preferred to claim, embarrassingly she felt – 'the making of her'.

The car she parked that evening was barely three months old: brilliant white with cream leather seats and a burgundy trim; pleasingly, vulgarly sporty.

The coolly luminous dashboard dimmed smoothly to darkness and she paused to gather her thoughts. Used to being in a hurry, she was now faced with an event she had barely paused to consider.

It was warm in her car and the street looked cold. There was a five- or ten-minute walk to the restaurant.

And why – she challenged herself – had she dressed as if for a special occasion? A heavy black Italian skirt of meticulously textured wool that came to just below her knee; aubergine stockings and frankly wild heels in black veau velour and tonal fishnet that reeked of excessive expense. At least her top – a light-fawn jersey embroidered with a single thick black and off-white zig-zag line beneath the bust – was reasonably understated.

But then there was her totally berserk Missoni coat – gay-bachelor soft tweed in tawny-gold, black and tangerine check, with deep patch pockets and multi-colour knit sleeves in anthracite and vermilion . . .

Had she wanted to draw attention to herself, to make a statement of some kind, she could not have done a better job.

But even as she inwardly protested, out of patience with herself, she was looking forward to the evening.

It had been a long time since Marilyn had thought about meeting men. The long mothering years. And when had she last tried to make an impression? She had no idea. Now, out of nowhere, she was involved with Thomas.

Maybe she just needed to feel admired, desirable?

'Front, dear, front,' Julian used to tell her during the first year after Martin had left; meaning that she must keep up appearances at all costs. But had she ever – she dwelt cautiously on the irony – done anything other than keep up appearances?

Her mother had remarked, to her immediate irritation, that such was the principal occupation of 'une femme d'un certain âge'.

Marilyn glanced at herself in the rear-view mirror and shook her hair, dipping her chin as she did so. Her dark eyes looked back up at her, their expression soft but emphatic.

It was her hair that Thomas had first complimented. She was still not quite sure how he had managed it – a conversational sleight of hand.

His forwardness had been excused by his charm, which had made light-hearted the fact that in effect he was asking her out on a date.

It had all been done with utmost respect and good humour. He had succeeded, before she really knew what was happening, in creating an infectious appeal to his suggestion. How could such a delightful plan be anything other than pleasant and interesting – acquaintances becoming friends? There was no sordid edge; everything was relaxed, courteous.

Marilyn, despite her considerable surprise, had tried to maintain her reserve. Then at the last minute she had laughed and he got the full force of her famously lovely smile.

It was this smile that Thomas had taken away in his thoughts from the villa on Primrose Hill. On his way to dinner in town he had called by one of Josephine's soirées for the Friends of Wagner. Marilyn had been a complete surprise.

The smile won you over, so frank and open and warm – accompanied by sudden brightness in her eyes. Irresistibly it flattered its recipient, as if admitting them to a very exclusive club. Thomas had also noticed the perfecting dash of a manly or boyish quality in this sudden animation of Marilyn's expression. An openness and tantalising sliver of knowingness, possibly flirtatious – as if he had passed a first test.

Sitting in her car meanwhile, Marilyn felt suddenly hemmed in by circumstances. But what had she got to complain about? She looked out at the dark street, London so familiar. Thanks to her mother she lived in a Georgian terrace not ten minutes' walk from King's Cross station. And she always seemed to be busy . . . She had, she thought, a good relationship with Chloe. Her ageing parents needed her help.

Her father's birthday party came into her mind – Catherine had suddenly seemed a little brittle. But then she had slipped her arm around Marilyn's waist and given her a squeeze.

'Where are your parents? I must thank them . . .'

Perhaps it was all fine. Still she felt uneasy.

That had otherwise been a reasonable day, given the potential for calamities, which had been considerable. Her father, coaxed by applause, had made a short speech.

Bill was no longer the firecracker – setting off anecdotes and outrageous statements, delivering cultural bulletins, telling parables of modern life. That afternoon in the study, surrounded by friends and colleagues, some of whom he had known since the fifties, he had suddenly looked truly old. Not young-old, which her parents had seemed for decades, but visibly failing; his faculties weakened, his life force nearly spent.

His few words had opened uncertainly and obscurely.

'I was first impressed by a short film called *Gala Day*.' His voice was faint, huskily quavering. 'It was a marvellous piece about the Durham Miners' Gala.

It was not uncontroversial and taught by example. It ends with the people singing "The Red Flag".'

He chuckled.

Some of his listeners smiled; others looked slightly bewildered, trying to place his tone.

Marilyn meanwhile had noticed some drips or stains on the front of his pullover; also, that he was speaking so quietly. Then he had said something about the 1980s.

'Such terrible politics and even worse furniture.'

A loyal ripple of laughter.

'But every day seemed to bring new books and magazines and papers to my desk – nearly all of them interesting.' A glimmer of his younger self accompanied these words – a gathering certainty. 'Some of you may remember – that feeling, for us, of a big, exciting and important discussion that was going on weekly, daily . . .'

Abruptly, Marilyn saw again the dark, low-ceilinged kitchen at their old family home in Greenwich – the pompously named Captain's House; and how when she and Carmen were teenagers it had seemed that most weeks there were gatherings around the big table of these clever, busy people – the 'us' to whom Bill referred.

They had always just published something or just been on television or been about to be collected by cars from the BBC – to commentate and give their opinions, talk about their books.

She had never known people so determined to talk. It had made her want to scream, even then.

Then her father spoke about newly troubled times – the increasing need for vigilance. That the important conversation must continue. His warnings were met with a silence, it had seemed to Marilyn, that was more polite than attentive.

She had always felt excluded from the big important discussion and anyway was indifferent to it. Carmen, livelier, might have managed to hold the attention of all the clever people – if only for a few minutes; be able to amuse them with her precocity or flirtatiousness. Some of these public intellectuals had not been above having wandering eyes, wandering hands even.

But Marilyn, reserved by nature, had lacked both vivaciousness and the makings of a fine mind. Popularity with the elect and enlightened was not in her bargain. No smiled offers of unadvertised openings in cosy little publishing houses or fashionable television production companies had ever come her way. Her pedigree may have been immaculate – wealthy metropolitan cultural aristocracy – but she simply wasn't the right type.

Her modern world was shopping and the search for nice things; and then her world had been shopping for nice things with Martin. And thus she had been invisible to the participants in the big important discussion.

Now there was clapping and raised glasses and Bill was shuffling back to his place beside Josephine. He looked to Marilyn like a little boy. Age had shrunk, stooped and hollowed him. She wondered, had her love for him faded as well? She felt rather bloodless towards the whole occasion – couldn't find her feelings about it.

She thought of her own strength, health and fitness. Carmen, across the room – as always in a circle of friends and acquaintances and so assured – Carmen, to be honest, looked heavy. In ten years or less she'd be living in kaftans. But she carried it quite well. She had unthinkingly lit a cigarette, was blowing smoke up towards the ceiling, oblivious or indifferent to the disdainful looks she was attracting.

At the end of the hall there was a black-and-white photograph of Bill taken by someone famous in the early 1960s. In those days he looked like a young rugby player in his fisherman's jersey and leather jacket; his stare so clear-eyed and confrontational, a filterless cigarette hanging from the corner of his mouth. An overcast day, some blurred old buildings in the background . . . bomb sites . . .

'It all begins with ruins,' he had once written, 'doing the twist in a ruin.'

Then, across the accelerating years, the accomplishments and gathering fame, the daily drama of the exciting discussion; all the projects and meetings and reviews and dinners and lunches in Soho and Covent Garden; the deadlines and previews.

Now, the watery eyes and stains on the pullover; slowly climbing the stairs rather early; a gluttonous, touchingly sly fondness for childhood treats – cakes and ice creams. And the hotly debated magazines lost or yellowing, the learned journals slipped down the back of a shelf; the once important books for the most part forgotten; a box somewhere crammed with old VHS tapes.

71

And now his daughter was sitting in her new car; half wishing that she had not agreed to meet Thomas for dinner that evening at what she was sure would be the too grand and too dark Italian restaurant of a big hotel.

She pulled on her fine scarlet leather gloves. Taking her small smart bag off the passenger seat, she stepped out of her car and started to walk briskly towards Portman Square.

'Diaghilev in Thornby Avenue . . .'

Martin remembered Hannah's pronouncement. Marilyn had not heard her. His elegant wife had been standing at the long table, wearing a short-sleeved black tunic dress that showed off her tan. She was holding a bright silver serving spoon in one hand and concentrating on serving dessert.

They had been having lunch – one of the long summery lunches that Marilyn loved to prepare, served on the flawless dining table. The impressive and lovely inherited painting – a portrait of a lively flushed-cheeked young woman, her hat at an angle – watched over them from above the fireplace. The three broad sash windows, in a line, were all open to their serene expensive view.

Hannah was wearing a sleeveless black dress; three broad amber bracelets slipped with a light clatter down her long white arm. She was smoking cigarettes with white filters. The ragged little flags of silver-blue smoke drifted to one side, carried on the faintest breeze from the open windows.

It was a Saturday in July, the weather warm and humid – the view across the city from Clifton hung with a fine mist; a strong scent of grass and green leaves mixed with the smoke from Hannah's cigarette. Martin, finer-featured then, so much slimmer, had talked about London, about being a teenager – brought up between the country and the city, both within reach but neither truly attainable.

Hannah, staring out at the view, had raised her eyebrows but said nothing.

Marilyn had served Niçoise salad from a large pale-blue bowl that was prettily painted with pale-yellow and pink flowers. A Venetian decanter and water glasses, striped royal blue, deep red and yellow. A very cold bottle of Chablis, a second bottle chilling.

This was when Chloe was still a little girl. Dolls, soft toys, cartoons. When – '95, '96? The old world was still intact in those days – all comfortably in its place. Bill and Josephine endlessly busy and quietly celebrated. The noted Marxist film-maker and his wife the expert on Wagner; recently returned from their sojourn in California – politically provoked, they had loudly lamented in print and in person – back to London life and the Regency villa on Primrose Hill.

In America both had prospered; and now, in the warm sun that still shone upon them, they could enjoy their book launches and openings and premieres; the drinks parties at which all the guests were fine-minded people of note, so at ease in those days with their achievements and prizes, their household names and

73

newspaper columns, exotic travels, museum direct-orships; retreats in Puglia, converted watermills in Burgundy . . .

And Martin's mother, thinner, more easily tired, would be at home in Thornby Avenue – the house was still neat and fragrant then, if a little more faded and frayed. Hardly anything had changed there since Martin smoked his first cigarette, that mild afternoon.

There he had once drunk his jasmine tea and listened to the end of Fauré's Requiem Mass and developed his theory about depressed public schoolboys; leant out of his bedroom window to inhale an evening filled with the scent of fallen leaves.

The ordinary bedroom that he had made the museum of himself was also his carefully constructed film set. Violet light. The tenebrous atmosphere of falling dusk and church choral music and cigarette smoke. In his head, figures frozen in spotlit pale pink and pale blue against the blackness of a cavernous sound stage. His antique silver-grey tie, flecked with exquisite pinpoints of scarlet silk thread.

There was the magazine signed by Andy Warhol – a portrait of Mariel Hemingway on the cover; and the amber cigarette holder; his *Ludwig* film poster; and Jane Aire and the Belvederes – 1978, 'Yankee Wheels' / 'Nasty . . . Nice', eerie, mournful pleading chant; music of the nuclear industrial eventide, Akron, Ohio – all the way to Thornby Avenue.

★

When Marilyn pushed her way into the small crowded entrance of the famous Italian restaurant – there at the side of the big hotel – she was struck how the darkness within was midnight-blue and velvet-soft; also by the smiling graciousness with which the manager – a lady in late middle age wearing a severe charcoal-grey suit, her long hair swept up into a bun on the back of her head – seemed to know exactly who she was and whom she was meeting; by the sense of being enfolded in a private and luxurious world that wordlessly assured her that she was in her right and proper place.

She cut a more impressive figure than she imagined. Despite her earlier misgivings, what Julian would have called her 'inner wardrobe' had guided her to the correct outfit for the occasion. Tall in her extravagant evening shoes, in a setting where the almost invisible strip of scarlet brocade down their back seam would be noticed and appreciated, Marilyn shivered off her coat. It tumbled expensively and fragrantly into the waiting arms of a young female attendant, uniformed in pinstripe trousers, white shirt and black tie.

Every member of staff in that thrilling dim blueness could not have looked more delighted to welcome her, serve her, accept her as not just correct but . . . simpatico . . . Even the film-star-handsome young barman, curly-haired and blue-eyed, so expertly busy with bottles and glasses, looked up to flash her a smile and offer a friendly 'Good evening!'

The main room opened up before her in warm golden light. Opulent Italian chic; the eternal mid-century modern: heavy marble, heavy glass, heavy furnishings; in a style part private bank, part grand hotel.

Smoked-bark leather banquettes lined two of the walls, with long important-looking abstract paintings above them. In the centre were circular tables dressed with heavy white cloths, their silverware glinting beneath golden teardrops of candlelight. Further away, two carefully spotlit tables for four or six. Where, wondered Marilyn, did one find dinner candles such a delicious shade of ivory?

The restaurant, as always, was crowded. The diners, Marilyn noticed, were nearly all her own age or older. Just one or two very young women were apparent, their dresses too short and too clinging, in Marilyn's opinion; their jewellery excessive.

The men were all dressed in either dark suits or lounge suits. They had an international air of owning property in several countries, of being constantly and comfortably in transit . . . Always on to the next pleasure, the next acquisition, next aggrandising occasion.

They sought only the company, most of them, of people who increased their status – who brought something to the table, as it were; be that best of all an aristocratic, old or famous name, or great wealth, glamour or personal beauty; at the very least – lowest entry level – a talent to amuse.

Their age and demeanour brought to mind mansions and palazzi in Rome, Athens or Milan; baronial houses in old New York and vast white apartments in Tel

Aviv – all Bauhaus and bullet holes and poetically peeling wrought-iron trellises, there in the evening shadow of dusty palms. And everywhere, like a chord, hung Switzerland.

Marilyn noticed that several people – men and women – looked up at her as she was led across the room. A man slab-faced with senatorial presence wore the expression of trying to place her socially. Ought she to be known? Another, younger, his snow-white napkin tucked into his collar to spread flawlessly across his shirt front, paused open-mouthed to watch her as he raised his soup spoon to his lips.

At their prominent yet secluded corner table Thomas had already risen to his feet.

How does he do it? thought Marilyn. For before she could negotiate the moment he had rested his hand on her arm with the lightest pressure, leant forward to one side and given her a purely ceremonial kiss. The moment was enhanced by his ability – like that of a veteran comedian – to prompt laughter without seeming to do anything . . . It was something to do with his eyes, his smile – and above all, weirdly, his glasses.

'Ah, lovely, lovely!' he was saying. 'This is so nice. Such a pleasure to share something nice with you.' He gestured happily to her seat. 'And how was your father's birthday party? I remember the house!' He looked heavenwards and patted his sternum with his right hand – 'Really – so pretty.' Adding vaguely, 'And not an area I know . . .'

A white-jacketed waiter appeared, bowing slightly, his hands parted in welcome, as though anything they might desire could be theirs.

Thomas glanced at Marilyn and she saw again the face of a regal clown; one of ancient lineage – 'What will you take?' His accented voice was suddenly more apparent.

Marilyn could feel herself slipping into the prosperous world, so easeful and obliging, that Thomas inhabited. A place of significant antiques and . . . money, neither pure nor simple, as Thomas himself had once said.

They had met perhaps eight or ten times, over so many months; twice for long weekends.

'Negroni!' he said suddenly, raising one finger with an air of triumph as though he had just remembered the correct answer to a riddle. Marilyn nodded and smiled. Julian came to mind again: 'When in doubt, nod and smile.'

The couple idled pleasantly in small talk. Yes, her journey had been easy; no, she could not remember having been to this restaurant before, but of course she knew of it. How nice that Thomas could come from Paris to London on this trip. And what—

Their drinks arrived in heavy glass tumblers. 'To you,' Thomas said.

Marilyn smiled and inclined her glass very slightly towards him. As she did so her chin dipped again, just a fraction, and she glanced up at him over her drink for a second – looking directly into his eyes.

Thomas felt his answering gaze overwhelmed, pinned by her look and wondrously so. She was truly lovely – but more . . . As the alcohol warmed his throat and stomach he realised again the intoxicating power of Marilyn's effect on him.

Marilyn would never say so to anyone, but Thomas removed the need for thought. And he was kind; and fun, in his own way. She could be with him and in her own world. She looked good and enjoyed being quiet.

'Guess what,' said Chloe.

'Tell me now.'

'My mother's seeing her boyfriend tonight.'

Alice leant against the ivory-white wall in the high-ceilinged hallway. A tarnished oval mirror in a chipped gilt frame was level with her shoulders. She wore very dark denim – jacket and jeans – that looked heavy and stiff. A blood-red paisley scarf as a cravat. Her reddish hair, very straight, came down to her shoulders.

'That's nice.'

She didn't sound particularly interested. But Chloe had been trying to recall her low voice, the intonation slightly flat; to hear it in her head, for days.

Just then Alice took a step forward, put an arm around Chloe's shoulders and pulled her towards her, kissing her full on the lips. Chloe caught the smoky scent of her richly ecclesiastical perfume; enjoyed the sudden strength of her embrace. The rough denim grazed her cheek.

This was the second time that Alice had been to the house. On the first occasion, drunk and late at night, she had seen very little of it. But enough to recognise that it was not a typical shared house, with bikes in the corridor, bright overhead lights, scuffed white walls and all the naked apparatus of living, exposed and ugly. Not that, most definitely. This house spoke lazily but clearly of inheritance.

Three walls of the square drawing room were painted dark blue. An ancient bookcase rose nearly to the height of the ceiling along the back wall. Dotted about the room were two or three elderly small circular tables, marked with drink rings and cigarette burns. A scattering of low-shaded lamps gave off their dimmed warm light; two old club armchairs could be seen in the shadows, their leather pungent and cracking. In the bay of the window was another sofa, battered but grand. And antique cushions everywhere: dark colours, fringed and tasselled, tapestry or satin, limp with age.

Old things from big houses.

Just Chloe and her friends Janine and Izzie made use of this sizeable Edwardian house – that was screened from the quiet street by a regularly tended beech hedge. In the small paved courtyard a leafless dwarf tulip tree awaited the spring.

This evening Chloe had the house to herself. She sat on the arm of the big, shabby but sumptuous sofa. Her white shirt and navy trousers looked sharp and fresh against the faded green silk stripe of the cushions. She moved fluidly, with the easy self-assurance of privilege. Two days a week she worked in some vague secretarial capacity for a philanthropic trust, just off Eaton Square; had a barely formed plan to study botany . . . horticulture . . .

The second time she saw her, at a party, Alice had swept her off her feet.

Alice alone made her feel coquettish – flippant and mercurial. The way she always looked like she was about to leave a room or situation, not giving a reason and with silent restlessness.

When she relaxed, in private, Alice became luxurious. At that moment, to Chloe, the thought of losing her was terrifying. Doing anything at all with her was the most exciting thing in the world. She longed to serve her, to hold her attention.

Alice had asked about her parents.

On the low table in front of the sofa were two glasses of white wine and an old Manila envelope – one of the 'circulation envelopes' that they used to have in offices, with a grid of boxes printed on the front for each recipient to initial. Some contained illegible signatures; others were authoritative, neatly dated. It was fastened with a strand of waxed cotton, coiled around a circular cardboard disc. Decades old, the sturdy brown paper had become soft and smooth, almost furred. It had the dried-out airless smell of old cardboard.

'Dad had kept these.'

Carefully unwinding the string, Chloe pulled out a clear plastic wallet, with holes for filing punched down one side. She withdrew a sheaf of old photographs, postcards, contact strips and Polaroids with cold bluish chemical hues; even one or two business cards from shops long gone. The address – '77 King's Rd' – stood out on one of them: a hairdressing salon, the height of fashion forty years earlier, its name printed as though coolly dashed off in shocking pink felt-tip, slick and sleek.

'Do you mind me looking?'

'No – I want you to see them. Dad said he'd like to see them again but then he forgot. He probably doesn't even remember the conversation.'

Alice was looking at a contact strip: four tiny oblong images in black and white. There was young Martin. So skinny, wearing a white or cream double-breasted jacket with a pale and shiny t-shirt beneath it. He was with a girl dressed in black who had short black hair and wore heavy make-up. Her arm was slipped through his. In one of the photos she was miming the act of vomiting. In another she was looking at Martin with extraordinary tenderness. They were standing beside a bar in a plain, brightly lit room.

'I have no idea who that is,' said Chloe. 'And everything looks so – Soviet.'

Alice picked up one of the Polaroids.

'Mum,' said Chloe.

Alice had always thought Polaroid suited the modern past – was its native tongue. The greenish-white and pale-blue light. Just as oil painting, in the right hands, not only depicted grandeur and pathos but achieved them.

And here was Polaroid love. Young Marilyn seated on a low boxy sofa upholstered in moss-green velveteen. She was leaning back, laughing, but did not look at ease. The wall behind her was bare, lit up by the crude camera flash to a shade of milky off-white.

'That's my dad's old house,' Chloe said. 'I mean, his mother's house.'

'Your mother's so lovely,' said Alice.

'You think so?'

'She knows that she's incredibly sexy but she doesn't know if she wants to be.'

'Heavens.'

Marilyn would have been in her early twenties then. One of her rare visits to Martin's native suburb. It had been a very warm summer; the Thames at Greenwich torpid. She had cut her hair and dyed it white-gold; exchanged her demure North London prettiness for something modern and flashy.

In the photo she was laughing, her eyes bright, but her posture was stiff. One arm was brought up across her chest, her young brown hand nervously clenched; the other lay across her lap. She was wearing a white skirt and what looked like a silk pyjama jacket, white with vertical gold stripes.

'Quite the looker.' Alice lit a cigarette. 'But old photographs – they wear you out. It's like they're using up our lives because theirs are over.'

★

Though modest, Marilyn knew she could look striking. Six months earlier she had questioned herself: did she want to have an adventure – an encounter? Or did she want to leave?

No, not to leave, most definitely.

It had been years, likewise, since she had drunk aperitifs. Now, firmly but kindly, the negroni melted the knots of tension in her neck and shoulders.

The conversation was so pleasantly undemanding. Thomas was talking about Paris – how he preferred Brussels: 'Lovely grey rainy Brussels,' he said. Marilyn remembered the high front of his elegant town house; the enormous bow windows on the ground and first floors; all so grand yet understated.

He had told her that the English had not known elegance since the eighteenth century.

The proposition was of no great interest to her; but she thought as he was speaking about the soft thickness of his doubled shirt cuff – the shirt had a fine navy stripe – and the weight of his gold cufflinks. She felt the charisma of age with substance.

He had ordered some white wine to begin; and then – 'Something quite big . . .' – a red for later: Piedmont . . . Südtirol . . .

She very gently pushed a strand of hair behind her ear and smiled as he told her some inconsequential story about his week. His manners were impeccable; the exquisitely phrased and extravagant compliments so deftly inserted at every turn in the conversation, yet never cloying.

84

When she replied – bits and pieces of small talk – she felt as though her life was echoing.

But she noticed, not without pleasure, that while she spoke her admirer did not take his eyes off her. He was studying her, serious for the first time that evening.

She made him laugh, saying about herself, 'Other than linguine with Cornish lobster, I have absolutely no idea what happens next.'

Then she smiled again, and gave her suitor a quick wink.

Six

There were the double escalators going down to the vast lobby of the building where Martin worked – a tower so big and new it didn't have a name.

A long reception desk, brilliant white laminate, stood at a slightly oblique angle to the wall. The two receptionists were men in late middle age who seldom smiled. They wore a uniform of dark suit and navy-blue tie embossed with a small silver crest. One had a headset and earpiece; both wore heavily framed glasses. Behind them, on the soaring white marble wall, hung an enormous assemblage of randomly shaped sections of powder-pink and royal-blue plastic, pushed into a haphazard configuration.

Martin descended that cold Thursday night buttoning his overcoat. The lobby was deserted, with only the night receptionist on duty. He was looking down at his computer screen, absorbed. The lenses of his glasses were filled with reflections of white light. He did not look up as Martin walked by.

Pushing himself out into the street, Martin walked very slowly towards Moorgate, his hands deep in his coat pockets and his chin pushed down into his scarf. That slightly feverish weariness . . . It didn't want to shift. A lingering hangover, like jet lag. The evening crowds hurried past him in the opposite direction, on their way to Liverpool Street station.

Martin often went to the same restaurant, housed in the glass-walled building that bridged London Wall. There in saffron half-light was the table he liked by the window; a view down to the dual carriageway that passed silently underneath. He found the contrast between the dim-lit warmth inside and the cold street outside, so close, especially enjoyable.

He and the table were old friends. It stood just slightly apart. If he sat facing west, the impression was of dining within a grove of illuminated glass towers that were pristine, secure and restful.

He had brought Chloe here once. 'These places are exactly like the kind of music you like,' she had said. 'Melancholy on the dance floor.'

That must have been at least a year ago, maybe two. It was good they were in touch again now. She always seemed busy; and Alice . . . He liked Alice – her attitude, everything . . . She reminded him a little of Gareth.

Had she and Chloe exchanged amused looks towards the end of the meal the previous night? He didn't really mind if they had. He had drunk more than both of them put together; but he had been careful, he thought, to keep mild-mannered, non-committal, light . . . 'Some semblance of dignity.'

It was good to be on his own tonight.

One or two of the restaurant staff knew him. They liked him because they trusted him – knew him to be courteous and generous, charming even. Taking his seat beside the glass wall, he ordered his usual large gin and tonic, a half-bottle of Chianti and a bottle of sparkling water. He knew the menu by heart – ordered as usual the Niçoise salad and some kind of melted-cheese focaccia, strewn with sea salt and rosemary, chilli oil . . . Soon a second half-bottle of Chianti . . .

After an hour or so, he was suspended, weightless, in a pause in time that was meaningful and poetic and enabled him to see immense distances. He simply had to stay forever in this stilled floating moment, in which everything was benign and comfortably significant.

He felt that he could see modern dim-lit corridors that led to quiet apartments; deserted street corners after rain had stopped; empty platforms and wide sodium-orange roads curving out of London – off towards the suburbs at night.

Somewhere out there – and he could see down the tracks, through an orderly, alluring nocturnal world of floodlit yards and vacant lots – far beyond, was his family home. His old room looking out over the Heath – as the common land that lay beyond Thornby Avenue was known locally; there were the wind-bent trees against the silver-blue evening sky.

This was the one true horizon, right now; and this

vista – familiar and comforting, while as desolate at dusk as any coastal spit of land, far from any village – brought memories of frozen Boxing Day snow, silent in the evening; the roads and avenues and cul-de-sacs all white and deserted. Somewhere through the cold the smell of woodsmoke. The haunting, wistful theme tunes of the television dramas they had back then.

His hand became clumsy as he reached for his glass; the red wine was rich and pungent.

Then, yes – the lunch party, that summer's day. A young bourgeois masque. Hannah, with the vacationing air of an off-duty attendant spirit, as Marilyn, bringer of order, served dessert . . . Deep-crimson summer pudding. Cold single cream from an antique jug.

Then he saw his old room again. Everything started with cigarettes. Outside was the modest cottage-style garden, pale-grey fence and neat lawn. An apple tree in blossom. In his eyes, forty years ago, a French impressionist meadow. Again he stared into the night, sipping the heavy red wine. The second bottle had gone rather quickly, and so . . .

He remembered the warm summer evenings, '74, '75, when Christine would come over and sit for hours on the beige, white and black Indian-print floor cushions from Import Cargo; smoke her mentholated cigarettes and talk about shopping and music and love. In stereo hi-fi the minimal floating tones, softly, steadily unfolding, overlapping, to merge with the dusk, the deepening green shadows at the end of the garden.

'Can I bring you anything else?'

The waitress was smiling down at Martin. He noticed her angled black pencilled eyebrows, white shirt and loosely knotted black tie. Modern synthesis; the hastily constructed bombshell. Her dyed blonde hair was pulled off her face with a broad black elastic hairband, to hang to one side in a sultry fright-wig style. He raised his glass with a smile.

'Large?' Chin lowered, she raised an eyebrow.

'That would be heaven.'

Understanding smile. Then she was gone, as though a hologram had been switched off.

Secure in the meaningful pause, seeing deep into the poetic world, Martin stared down at the car lights once more, scarlet one way, cold white the other. The pursuit of pleasure – he reminded himself, raising his glass to the night – had become a search for happiness. How proud he had been of the insight.

Drunk again, his feelings flowed, luxuriously unimpeded. Diaghilev . . . Diaghilev of the London suburbs . . . Before the wasted years; before *'it is the ease and frequency with which . . .'*

Memory. His actual job was remembering . . . That's right. These days.

And here was the large glass of red wine, to which the waitress had added a good deal extra.

'Glass and a half,' she said with a wink as she put it before him. Did she like him? Or was she treating him kindly, as you might an ageing lost cause or harmless casualty? God alone knew how he would feel in the morning; he would simply deal with it.

The morning was distant and he was the presiding spirit of the meaningful modern night, able to see for miles and miles – through buildings and the wide cold spaces of the London parks, through the concrete of the underpass . . . His the sovereignty of the outsider.

Of course, he had no interesting or exotic racial heritage, no great journey behind him, no cause to claim; had never been a witness to violent historic events – purges or coups, persecution and prejudice. Politics never more than a far-off background noise.

In the end all there was – and Martin, there in the blissful suspended moment, had the sensation that he was looking down from a height, as though from among the grimy iron rafters high above the concourse of Liverpool Street station – in the end *all* there was . . . was a cheap wicker chest, the size of a picnic hamper maybe, there in his sister's old room at Thornby Avenue. This held what was left of his record collection – just thirty or forty vinyl discs in their cardboard sleeves; but each a world, a chapter, a moment. Combined, a decision.

That was the hand he'd been dealt, so . . . That was just how it was . . . Streets and stations . . .

Through the low humming silence that was filling his head, aware of the lengthening delay between his thoughts and movements, he could see the wicker chest now, in the little back bedroom at twilight. How odd, how shaming maybe, that a basket in a sunbeam should contain the power source that had driven his life, at the very least shaped his decisions – perhaps even brought him to where he was sitting now . . .

Beyond that room in which the light was slowly thickening, the small suburban landing would be filled with bright summer-evening sunshine. In his thoughts, Martin walked silently towards his old bedroom door.

The door had been painted over the years with several coats of thick white gloss. It was inset with four elongated panels. There was a small brass knocker, set high and centrally, blackened now and impossible to clean. A Bakelite doorknob, as old as the house, the mechanism of which gave a loose metallic rattle when turned to the right to open the door.

Inside was a perfectly ordinary room, painted white, a little larger perhaps than you might expect and with a window that nearly faced the sunset – catching first the amber then pink declining rays at an angle, as they stretched and lengthened down the wall. The only feature was an old fireplace, long closed up, with a wooden mantelpiece painted the same many coats of gloss white as the door . . .

The vinyl records, once propped against the cool white wall, had pervaded his life with their own.

'. . . and that has to mean something,' he had said to Marilyn, in the earliest days of their love. They had been lying on Martin's bed, late one Sunday afternoon at his flat in Vauxhall. Marilyn, studying the shadows on the ceiling, only giving his musings a fragment of her attention yet still adoring him, had nodded, stroked his arm. In those days his voice was her home.

Now Martin turned his gaze away from the soundless dual carriageway, brought back to the urban low-light, melancholy-on-the-dance-floor of the restaurant, quiet contemporary, close by London Wall, dining alone.

He didn't care that he had revealed himself to be one of those who eats alone in order to drink unquestioned. The waitress knew already and she didn't care either – he was just one of several regular loners. He would cause no fuss and leave fairly soon with studied care or that particular unsteady heaviness . . .

'Could I have another glass of this, please – and the bill . . .'

The old plan, the therapy plan: to write to everyone and apologise for everything. The dreadful ways he had behaved, the letting people down, and mess . . .

In his old room he had nurtured a spindly fronded palm, suburban houseplant, in honour of the grand cafés of old Europe; and placed on the white mantelpiece a mirror in a varnished bamboo frame, art deco in style – the Hollywood Orient, Casablanca . . . *Taking Tiger Mountain* . . . Marilyn Monroe in black and silver.

The first time he had put his arm around Francesca's waist, as she lay there – incredibly, to him – one warm July evening; and felt the light hem of her cerise silk blouse, then the warmth of her back against the soft white underside of his forearm. She had been so happy, her arms and smile so welcoming, during those first few weeks.

And what had Hannah said, when he told her all this? Rashly, drunkenly . . .

'Stuck. You're so stuck.'

But she had been a good friend to both of them, over the years.

Rising slowly, his legs stiff, Martin saw that at least he was not the last to leave. He felt ungainly and coarse. As he pulled on his coat he knocked over his wine glass with the back of his hand – gave himself away, entirely; but couldn't be bothered to stand it upright. The dregs splashed over the tablecloth. He looked uncertainly towards the waitress but she either didn't see him or didn't smile. He walked too quickly towards the door.

Outside he stood for a moment and breathed in and out through his mouth. Something felt wrong, a pain. The drinking, most probably – two heavy nights in a row. The steely cold was sharp on his hands and face as he pulled on his gloves. There was the escalator going down to the street. Glass and concrete. Ice-blue light and shadows.

A film, he remembered – thirty, forty years old: a wild East End alcoholic; looked like a messiah who had stood too close to an explosion; staring, startled eyes; dirt and hair and beard; sitting on the steps of the old Wesleyan chapel. Shell-shocked by the blast of life.

Martin looked towards lights and people; the busy junction. Supernatural things happened in London all the time, he said to himself – even in broad daylight. That man he had seen who walked through a downpour without getting wet, for instance. There must have been some explanation.

'When you're young you have enough time to be with people you don't really care about one way or another,' Thomas was saying. 'Then you spend your thirties dropping most of the people you met in your twenties. And we all know the forties are terrible – ask anyone.'

The restaurant was quiet now, their corner table softly lit, surrounded by its moat of velvet-blue darkness; the little vase of fresh flowers, damson-red, minutely spotlit against the heavy white tablecloth.

They had shared the linguine, then rabbit with some kind of astonishing charred vegetables that Marilyn loved. They drank Barbaresco, rich, smoky and bewitching.

Then an espresso for Thomas, mint tea for Marilyn and for fun a glass of limoncello.

'I've enjoyed myself.' Marilyn said the words before she had thought about them.

Thomas raised his palms. 'I hope to see you again soon – as soon as you like.' His expression was soft and slightly sad – a gentle entreaty.

Her smile again, so warm.

Then he said, 'Tell me about your husband. We've never really talked about him. Unless you . . .'

'Oh – it's all a long time ago.' Marilyn spoke as though she didn't mind answering, but was surprised by the question. 'Another life. I was very young. We both were.'

'But you were together for some time?'

'Nearly twenty years, in all.'

It seemed as though she was bringing the subject to a close. Then she said, 'You go through so many phases with it. I don't know whether you felt the

96

same when you got divorced – I didn't find starting a new life easy.'

'Jasmine and I just didn't get on,' Thomas shrugged. 'We married in haste but did not intend to repent at leisure. So it was all quite easy – we both wanted out. But the money – the money was difficult.' He laughed. 'I kept the houses,' he added.

'We were very sure of ourselves,' said Marilyn, stroking one of the flowers very lightly with her fingertips. 'I was every inch the little bourgeoise my father was always terrified I'd become . . .'

Thomas found the word 'bourgeoise' on her lips utterly charming. It was so unlikely.

'He'd have been happier if I'd become a groupie. But really, we were so immature. I mean compared to my daughter, who's now the age we were then. A friend said we wanted "the whole kit". I was really annoyed at the time, but she was right.'

Thomas looked at the table and nodded. The sad sagacious acceptance of unalterable truths. But for him a comfortable sort of acceptance; many sunny terraces still ahead.

'They say most couples stay together for about seven years,' he said. Then he pulled a face, as if weighing ponderous odds – part gambler, part stooge of fate. 'Fair to say, *non*?' He looked at Marilyn and gave a brief, businesslike nod, as though to accept the estimate was good enough for them. He wanted to add 'I wonder how long we'd last' – but left the thought unspoken, to be savoured later as a digestif.

To him Marilyn was in the languorous July of her life. He was further along, but only a little. The Indian summer had not quite yet given way to autumn. And they had made one another laugh.

Age had given him confidence. Confidence to be happy and grateful for her company; to simply wait and see what might happen. For age, too, had made an honest man of him, more or less.

As the couple rose from their table, Martin was walking towards Liverpool Street station.

He found he could only walk short distances – ten, a dozen steps at a time, then was forced to stop. Not the pain in his legs this time, but an odd heaviness, tightening in his chest. He looked around, lifted his chin; tried to rejoin the hurrying late-night world.

The street was cold and busy. The sight of the crowds was exhausting and overwhelming – like a dam of great height up ahead, huge and grim in the dark; or as though he had to live the lives of everyone he could see.

People pushed by him as he stood in the middle of the pavement. He clutched the lapels of his overcoat and pressed his fist against his chest. Through his drunkenness there was a feeling of having no room left within himself. The thought of the future filled him with dread.

He moved uneasily, becoming more nervous. And the pressure, beneath where his black-gloved fist was clenched, was becoming pain more quickly – there, again. An odd scything heaviness, a spinning concrete wheel pushing into his chest and then making his jaw hurt, a spot of deep pain just to the left of his chin. He walked a few more paces; if he rested a moment . . .

He was now by the entrance to the station and could see down the crowded escalator to the noisy concourse below. That way lay the fresher air, higher up; the raised tracks and calm. To take deep breaths; survey the immense vista.

He sat on the shallow dirty steps outside the station, facing the street. Laughing and shouting people, deep in their evenings, flowed around him. No one looked at him. The street was filled with revellers, hastening couples, a few late commuters.

Martin closed his eyes, feeling feverish and unwell. There was the pressure; the pain.

. . . Stuart used to wait for him on the steps of St Paul's. During that last year before he disappeared, he would often be in his own world – drunk by lunch-time, on the roller coaster. Walking from side to side, his eyes closed, his head filled with the gale, holding a cigarette to his lips.

Once, Martin realised, he was reciting, chanting, singing to himself in his head – living in a world behind his eyelids, his chin jerking to an unheard beat. Then he would come back down to earth.

He had taken to wearing a shabby brown trench coat over his suit; his tie was twisted; his shoes had been repaired many times.

Sometimes they had gone to an old restaurant for clerks on Carter Lane – a dingy black-panelled room that had been there for decades; a place that now enjoyed a rather exclusive reputation. No bookings were taken; it was hard to get a table. It served school food; one claret, one burgundy, a bottled ale.

The high windows had reminded Martin of the classrooms at Tiles. There were tattered centrefolds on the back wall – pictures of nude girls on bikes. The place was run by an old army chef, an Australian. He would always ask, 'How's the special today, boys?' – going from table to table, always the same.

Martin looked up, trying to catch someone's eye. Pressing down on the step with one hand, he managed to stand. If he could get down to the concourse someone could help him. In his dusty black coat he stood by the top of the escalator. He found a place and began to descend. He felt a terrible anxiety that would not be quelled.

. . . The previous autumn, up towards Hackney Downs, he had noticed a regular gathering of elderly black men on a side road opposite a church – there beside the entrance to one of the big old red-brick estates. The dark bulks of the five-storey blocks were separated by floodlit courtyards. The flats had balconies and white-framed windows. There were tall trees along the length of the low wall, black and orange in the streetlight.

The old men would gather there once or twice a week in the misty early evening – smoking, drinking and laughing; sometimes dancing a few steps; the eldest seated on folding chairs.

From time to time younger men joined them; would park alongside, wind down the car windows; play shuddering oscillations of sound – crazily accelerated beats . . .

The party would last two, three hours.

Martin had felt drawn to the scene but had no idea why. Impossible for him to do anything other than pass by in silence, head bowed, to glance – walking slowly and heavily along the other side of the road, beside the church. Once or twice he had nearly crossed over, to approach, smiling . . . wanting to join in.

The smell came back to him: fallen leaves, smoke and skunk filling the damp night air; and around the foot of the nearest tree were night-light candles in little glass cups – pink and green and yellow glass, boiled-sweet colours; and a carefully arranged circle of empty bottles, placed there like precious objects: white rum, vodka. Some kind of shrine: a photograph wrapped in clear plastic of a shy family man, smiling, sitting in his neat living room . . .

A woman on the other side of the concourse caught sight of him. Something was clearly wrong, she thought, with the man at the foot of the escalator – a bulky man in a black coat, his face very pale.

He had turned to a young couple to say something. Now he was bending at the waist, reaching out towards the young man who tried to support him.

Another, older man had stopped. He had a briefcase under one arm – was resting his hand on the sick man's shoulder.

More people congregated around the event. One pulled out a phone – when suddenly the man in the overcoat fell, gave way and landed heavily on his left side.

The young couple backed away; the older man leant forward. He crouched down, looking at Martin's eyes. He looked up, shaking his head, not knowing what to think. Martin's expression was faraway, but he was conscious.

They wondered if he could be moved but didn't know – it felt as though some minutes passed, that he fell briefly asleep but surely had not; then he heard the loud abbreviated whoop of a siren.

Martin felt pain and faint. The station's dirty floor against his cheek – cold as marble, musty-smelling. And to not care where he was or what he looked like. It hurt to think about speaking.

Then a man and a woman; heavy bags thudding down beside him. Their voices sounded near and far away at the same time.

He could smell the London rain on the paramedic's jacket. Then a sudden freezing spray in his mouth. It tasted chemical, metallic. The pain eased slightly.

He let himself be turned, lifted. A low clattering trolley. Stared up at the dirty transparent jungle-canopy roof, dark now; the painted iron pillars; odalisques and water lilies.

But if he could feel the fresher, damper air on his face; see the wide vista from the elevated tracks; the new buildings and old streets.

Seven

'The decision has been made.'

The consultant's voice was deep, cultured; his tone grave yet lightly, reassuringly ironical.

Dr Howard pressed his fingertips together and was silent for a moment. Tall and lean with thinning hair and an aquiline profile, his presence inspired confidence. He was seated in the armchair opposite Martin's bed, scribbling down notes with his dark-green fountain pen.

His solemn expression conveyed the urgency of the situation. Then he spoke more briskly, in a muscularly assertive tone that Martin remembered from school.

'Once these things have been decided, it's best to get on with them.'

There was talk of where the problems were in Martin's heart – their severity, somewhat unusual presentation and unfortunate inaccessibility.

In the afternoon he returned with a quiet white-haired man. This was Mr Fox, the surgeon. He spoke little and addressed Martin as 'sir'.

Which was to say that Martin must have open-heart surgery.

'Or the consequences may be very serious.'

'How serious?'

'The first symptom would most probably be death.'

Martin felt strangely unmoved, then liberated. Here, suddenly, was a break from the circle; a way ahead, beyond the reach of everything. Nothing but acquiescence was required of him. His main concern now was how to avoid seeing anyone.

Early the following week he lay very still on his bed in one of the hospital corridors, looking up at white ceiling tiles. There were no windows but the light was that of earliest morning on an overcast day in late winter.

The previous night he had been given two sleeping pills. He hadn't slept well, he thought. Now he felt very different, deep in stillness.

In the dim wintry light of the long corridor he was aware of people around him. The bed started to move, steadily rolling forward. The corridor grew lighter; as though they had moved away from the overcast morning into broad daylight.

New people were around him now, younger and quicker; and it felt much cooler, almost cold. Classical music was playing very quietly – a Bach Cello Suite.

He suddenly felt the sharpness of the needle and tight transparent dressing of the cannula on the inside of his right elbow.

A dark-haired young woman dressed in green scrub top and trousers glanced first at him and then upwards, across the bright white room. Her expression was intensely alert. She briefly rested her hand on his shoulder.

'Another two point five milligrams.'

He felt a cold sensation in his arm and sudden calm flowing through his body; motionless serenity, almost sinking into himself.

A brief pause; then a row of plasma screens bumped into life and the people in the operating theatre looked up at them.

Gowned and masked, the consultant anaesthetist took a seat level beside him. Here was a pharmacology scholar, expert in oblivion.

'May I just look at your wrist?'

Very gently he took Martin's hand.

Then, nothing.

'So, you've been reborn,' said Hannah.

She was dressed differently, Martin thought. An open brown waistcoat over her green pullover; jeans, a blood-red and silver scarf.

Martin was lying on his bed. Much of the time he felt stilled, deep within himself; his thoughts slow and hazy. It was not an unpleasant feeling.

From a neighbouring room the pulse beat of a patient monitor could just be heard; and across the corridor, very faint, orchestral music.

'They've taken out some of the tubes,' he said, his voice low and quiet. 'I'm not sure what they were for.'

Hannah lifted his left hand very gently. She was studying the long incision down the inside of his forearm. It was strange to feel her careful touch.

She looked at the vertical wound in his chest and grimaced.

'And your leg?' He saw her concern. 'You said they took an artery from the inside of your leg?'

'Yes.'

She sat down in the armchair that faced the bed, noticing the neatness of the room and absence of personal belongings. There was something rather touching, she felt, about the neatness.

'You died during surgery.' She made it sound like an achievement.

'They run your heart and lungs through machines.'

'Even so . . . How do you feel?'

To Hannah he looked very pale, his cheeks . . .

'I feel strange – very tired.' He was slightly breathless. 'They make you start trying to walk again. And I've got fluid in my lungs. I can't breathe so well. I keep having X-rays.'

He was thinking how Hannah looked older for the first time in years; and less extreme. He always thought of her in black, in a bar or restaurant somewhere, and on guard.

He was about to say that he usually only saw her when he was drunk. But the words died, their spirit as much as their meaning expired; and with them, he fancied, a previous world in its entirety.

It had been dark midwinter, the freezing night when they first brought him in. Then, London had been cold and cavernous; dirty, street-lit and loud. Now, from his bed, Martin could see pale-blue sky; sunshine on the wiry colourless grass of a shallow slope. Still cold.

'Have you seen Chloe?' asked Hannah.

'Marilyn came to intensive care; and Chloe briefly. But I don't remember . . . I'd like to see Chloe.'

'I'm sure she'll be back soon. I know she wants to see you, very much.'

Martin felt sleepy; but seeing Hannah sitting across the room was restful and comforting.

'The surgeon says that I probably won't remember much of this,' he said. 'I think I will. It all feels very vivid.'

'Maybe you'll think that you remember it.'

'Maybe. It feels like everything has to change.' He closed his eyes.

The easeful sinking into himself, his breathing low and steady.

Hannah was writing in a notebook. She did look different. She glanced up at him and smiled.

'Have I been asleep?' asked Martin. 'I think I was dreaming.'

'Just for a few minutes.'

It had been nearly half an hour. Hannah put down her pencil. 'Have you ever heard of the first fall and second fall?'

'No, I don't think so.'

'I was reading about it. It's the idea that we have a crisis – that's the first fall – and we survive it. Your soul has been accosted; questioned whether it wants to stay in the body. So you get through that and think you've had a big epiphany. But then there's a second fall – and you're questioned again. And that's the one you've got to watch out for.'

Tired, his leg sharply painful, Martin found the theory obscure. There seemed no getting away with anything any more.

'What's the book?'

'Some long title – it's by a Buddhist. I'll find it for you.'

'I'd like to see it.'

Robert Groom . . . The Austrian count. He was a Buddhist. The count found a mouse in his flat in West London. He had driven with it from Barons Court to the Forêt de Meudon and there released it back into the wild – 'Just to be sure.' The nasal drawl. Crazy. Possibly untrue.

Hannah picked up her bag. 'I have to be off. But I'll come again soon.' She crossed the room and leant forward to kiss him. Again she looked different; like someone usually in uniform dressed in civvies. And she seemed so tall; her hair so long.

'You and me was ever friends,' she said, looking him in the eyes. 'And then, what larks . . .'

A joke from the long-ago days of old films, long weekends and late breakfasts.

She left the door ajar as he asked. When she'd gone he could see a line of yellowish overhead light in the corridor; hear the movement and low chatter of nurses. Outside the room a doctor was reading his file. His face dipped towards the page, expressionless.

At the beginning of Martin's second week in hospital Marilyn came to visit him.

His recovery had not been as swift as Dr Howard had hoped. Some breathing problems . . .

'Keep an eye on you for a few days,' he had said. Martin felt tired and peaceful; could not imagine leaving the quiet, closed routine just yet.

He had been thinking about Marilyn quite often, even before he was ill. All that they had once shared together. In recent years they had seldom met.

In his hospital bed he recalled an old film – some ballroom scene in a seaside town. A spotlight moved from couple to couple, eventually selecting the best pair of dancers. He imagined his life was the dancers; the spotlight the focus of his memory. And now it had settled on Marilyn and himself – he could almost see the two of them in watery monochrome; only too far away to hear him if he called.

Since the divorce, whenever he saw her his former wife had always been present but absent. That was the only way Martin could describe it. He knew very little about her life; gleaned bits and pieces of news from Chloe – but she never seemed to want to say much. What she did say was vague and brief, offered as merely speculative. Perhaps those were her mother's instructions.

As she grew older Chloe's voice had acquired a particular authority. Such clear and precise intonation; and anything other than fact was bad form. Also an ability to talk over someone, as though it was for their own good.

'I'm socially intimidated by my daughter,' Martin had said to Hannah the previous year.

'It's because she feels insecure,' said Hannah. 'I've watched her over the years and particularly more recently. She's trying to be like her friends. They all have that irritating posh loud thing. But she's not like that. I'm sure she's playing a part – trying to fit in. Or cover something up.'

'Playing a part . . .' Poor, poor Chloe . . . Martin had been suddenly alarmed; turning over the words as he stared through misty morning sunshine towards the grey building blocks of Canary Wharf. Then and there he had wanted to be with her, surround her with his love.

So he had taken her for dinner at the melancholy-on-the-dance-floor restaurant. Ritual cheerfulness, like sealed steel doors. When she said goodbye she seemed to leave quickly. The evening left him feeling uneasy. He tried to call her but she didn't answer.

'Some divorces are easy,' he had said to Stuart, over the river in Southwark, amid the bustle and flames and gin. 'Ours really wasn't. It was angry and sad and like being under a curse.'

'It's sometimes better if you just hate one another.' Stuart, always on hand, red-faced and beaming, with stalwart advice.

'I think they both really hated me.' Martin stared at his half-empty glass. 'And maybe they still do. But not as much as I hate myself.'

Stuart gave a little upwards nod and raised his eyebrows for a second; but said nothing. He looked unimpressed.

The waitress topped up Martin's drink as she passed by with a laden tray.

It had always been difficult to imagine Marilyn being angry. Violent emotion of any kind sat so uneasily with her reserve. One might picture her getting exasperated or losing patience with a wearisome situation; but anger . . .

In the far-off innocent past, for example – when life was a romantic comedy, years and years ago; and she dropped a dessert she'd spent hours making – a big glass bowl . . . There had been something . . . Martin barely dared articulate the thought . . . incredibly *sexy* about the collision between her neatness and the forces of chaos.

On that occasion, with whipped cream, fruit and shards of crystal still on the floor before her, she had leant against the kitchen wall, very still and silent, and slowly smoked a cigarette – something he had never seen her do before.

She had looked like a French film star watching a young mechanic.

But real anger, such as Martin had provoked when he made his fatal confession – that had been impossible to foresee.

Among the worst things about that terrible scene had been the pain and violence that Marilyn's fury inflicted on herself. Her orderly, cool, quiet world shattered like the crystal bowl; the life she had built so carefully – even if she could take six months to choose a cushion cover . . . Had they grown old together such traits would surely have become fond family jokes . . .

Such an imagining – as Martin had reflected many times, on platforms and trains, in restaurants and bars – confronted the home-wrecker, himself, with the immovable thought that suppose he had *simply forgotten* that disastrous encounter with Alison Hayes? Just pretend it never happened.

But it was impossible to wholly forget the hotel room in which he and Alison had fucked – there was no other word – surrounded by Empire-style furniture and gilt-framed fake engravings of botanical specimens. And how willingly they had pursued the preceding evening into mounting suggestiveness, as tawdry as it was alluring, there in the Polo Bar of the Westbury hotel.

Alison, chance-met in Regent Street – '*Oh, hello!*' – whom he had worked and flirted with, briefly and timidly, when? Ten, a dozen years earlier? When he had not known that Marilyn was pregnant . . .

Over four or five hours the evening had become a succubus; he, playing the man about town, unable to draw back from her flirtatiously mocking, lightly oiled compliments – each one a dare. Both of them editing their lives to allow the sleazy dance to continue. The intimate darkness of the spacious bar had conjured an illusion of some vague international anywhere . . .

And thus Martin's life with Marilyn had reached its end – as if in darkness, he felt.

Now he lay on his hospital bed, barely moving, staring at the wall. The low-ceilinged room was restful.

He had come to like the private hospital deep in Surrey's leafiest suburbs; his treatment there being paid for by the office. He looked forward to the menu delivered each morning; the painkillers, kind nurses and muffled sounds of the day; the quiet of afternoon.

In such reverie, Marilyn had become a new Marilyn. He saw the two of them, neither reunited nor still apart, but together as individuals; and they were somewhere . . . like Amsterdam. Yes, on the quiet waterfront, Eastern Docklands; an immense temperate tranquillity; empty wharves and the calm broadening expanse of water, the vista unbrokenly flat beneath mild and blousy enormous skies.

Modern apartments of clean restrained design, symbolic of renewal. He and Marilyn were walking slowly, arm in arm, sometimes silent and sometimes talking, unhurried. The autumn sun still held some warmth. So much to catch up on.

Couples reunited, after all; and Hannah had said he was reborn, or had died and now was alive again.

Then, in the middle of the midweek afternoon, Martin saw the door open a few inches, cautiously.

'Hello?' Soft and enquiring, the unmistakable slight rise in Marilyn's husky voice.

The door opened a little wider and she entered the room. Coming over to his bed, she briefly squeezed his hand.

'How are you?'

Immediate conflict, unspoken but undeniable. Her tone was concerned but faked, he felt; masking only unshakeable indifference.

'Still here . . . Thank you for coming by, again.'

She was dressed so correctly yet so noticeably, as ever. A grey woollen skirt that came down to mid-calf; the brown Spanish riding boots beneath it; a worn-in grey jacket, Bavarian style, with cartridge pockets, horn buttons and rounded velvet collar; this worn over a white polo neck sweater that came so close to being provocatively tight – but also inferred some idea of equestrian propriety. In her hand was a big bunch of keys and digital fobs. A rich person's keys.

She sat down on the edge of the chair, there but not there. There, perhaps, for the sake of good form – to remain unimpeachable; while seeing right through him and no longer being shocked, or even surprised, by what she saw there.

'You came to intensive care,' said Martin. 'I'm afraid I can't remember anything about it.'

'Yes – Chloe came with me but only I could go in. They were quite strict. Do you have any idea when—'

As he looked at Marilyn, wearing clothes he had never seen before, so deep within her own world, Martin realised how far away in her past he now lay. Amsterdam disappeared, barely noticed. A life had gone by, it felt, since the flawless dining table, Julian and Paul; their old flat in Bristol a galleon setting sail through the night, and so on.

Now was the season of the elevated tracks and broad East London streets . . . The misty darkness and cosmically liturgical churches . . .

In that moment Martin saw beyond Marilyn to Cambridge Heath Road, Mare Street, Hackney Central, the big old Pembury Estate. And Marilyn's world—

'How is your father?' he asked.

'Oh, he's slowed down a lot this last few months' – her smile was sad but accepting. 'I think they're going to get a live-in carer. They're talking about it.'

On their money as on islands.

'I think a lot about him. I've never felt quite so overawed by someone as the first time I met him.' Martin realised he sounded too familiarly reflective, but: 'Your mother casually remarking how he argued with Joseph Beuys . . . I made such a fool of myself.'

'No . . .'

Her smile looked forced, a touch of indifference left unconcealed.

Shared reminiscence was out of the question. The border between them had been closed for so long that even the barbed wire was overgrown, subsumed in brambles. Guard towers glimpsed through copses of silver birch trees.

But there was the big kitchen in Greenwich, vivid in Martin's memories; a paper bag filled with little cakes topped with yellow icing, bought by young

Marilyn that morning in anticipation of his first visit to her home.

'Such a great colour,' Bill had said, taking one.

Martin had been so entranced, so thrillingly, dazedly falling head over heels in love with the big jovial public intellectual's quiet younger daughter.

Now, thirty-three years later, she sat before him, so stylish and so clearly eager to leave. Would there be a single moment, the beat of a second even, when they would catch one another's eye and be honest?

'But you're okay otherwise?' she asked.

The question seemed absurd. It was hard to know whether to answer truthfully or simply follow suit, taking the path of least resistance: a smiled reassurance that all was well.

Martin was about to tell her the truth — that he could see no good in himself; wanted to apologise to everyone for everything etc. — when he heard her take a breath.

'I have something to tell you,' she said. 'I don't know if this is the right time but I thought it was important to let you know before you see Chloe.' She paused, her cheeks flushing slightly. 'I'm getting married.'

Gareth, a head taller than most of those crowded around him, pushed sideways towards the bar. Martin followed. All around them were young men drinking pale lager from brittle plastic glasses.

It was late September 1979. Outside the sun was slowly setting, the street still warm.

The ceiling seemed to press down on the heads of the crowd. Hundreds of shouted conversations; the music playing over the PA. Martin looked around at the young men. Some were baby-faced, some gaunt; others, mostly with girls, raucous and laughing. Charity shop raincoats and old leather jackets; some black-dyed or peroxide messed-up hair. No small number looking as though absolutely *nothing had happened* since 1974.

A few characters around the edges, alone or in pairs, with their own strange homespun looks – monkish, paranoid, aloof.

As far as Martin was concerned, he and Gareth were simply sharper, more intense than the rest. They looked unclassifiable, he felt, up to date. Reactionary was the new radical; to look exaggeratedly conformist but remote – that was the idea; and the modern should be laced with nostalgia for archaic visions of the future.

Thus, severe haircuts like Weimar bank clerks or young starry-eyed Midwestern seminarians. Grey trousers, short-sleeved shirts; plain narrow ties, old-fashioned lace-up shoes. As though you sat alone for days in a bare room, terrified or plotting.

Gareth drank vodka, took speed and barbiturates. His disquieting claim to always be armed; of having studied the art of being impossible to remember.

Of aesthetics, he pronounced, 'The number of pillars in a temple should be less than the number of trees in a forest but more than can be counted.'

Martin, then not quite twenty years old, a cigarette hanging from the corner of his mouth, took strength from suburban order. So long as he was tethered to that placid landscape he was able to venture deep into the city – find its obscure and darker creases, study shades of acute romance.

Whatever he found there the old commuter train would always return him to his dim suburban station and the quiet roads beyond; to that familiar haven, a cup of tea and a cigarette, where routine and respectability shut out any poltergeists, such as Gareth, that might have followed him home.

There was a scattering of ragged applause and a few cheers. The musicians setting up on the small stage were unsmiling, young and intent. They paid no attention to the audience; began to play, indeed, as though no audience was present.

Firstly instrumental, swinging and darkly alluring; the guitar, bass and drums like rolling black waves at night; then autumnal, crepuscular, portentous – thunder at twilight.

The rhythms accelerated, becoming violent. The skinny singer's short brown hair sat in a high ragged fringe across his pale forehead. His smooth face and almost colourless eyes seemed those of a drugged angel. He looked unwell, heavily medicated; his skin clammy. He sang in a deep, desperate voice with his eyes closed – as if he could barely open them; then stared blearily up into the lights, unseeing.

Dressed in an open-necked grey shirt and grey trousers, his appearance was drab and clerical. Bent at the elbow, his arms jerked and flailed. He pushed away the microphone stand, looking as though he was about to lose consciousness. His frame seemed to shudder, his body jolting into convulsive movement. A shell-shocked automaton. His eyes were wide open now and staring, as though faced with some horror that only he could see.

Twirling a finger, he had pointed at the side of his head, singing faster, almost screaming. Then, as the music tumbled to silence, he turned away with the look of one defeated, all hope lost.

Eight

Six weeks passed. The April afternoon was sunny and mild. Encouraged to exercise, Martin made his way daily towards the Royal Exchange. He walked slowly and cautiously, with a stoop. The wound on his chest was still healing.

In the monochrome days of the early 1980s there had been evenings that drew him deep into this same maze of streets and alleys and courtyards, looking for something extraordinary – the start of a great love, an epiphany. He no longer believed in such mirages.

Behind him lay the street where he had first been taken ill. Ahead, the bench that was his destination.

All around were the banks and offices and old insurance companies; the perfunctory classicism and imperial pomp he had worked amid for years.

They looked less imposing now, these old buildings, as if ashamed of what they had become. A good many had been turned into bars; others were empty. Through tall Victorian windows he could see the big offices and old banking halls, unlit, some partitioned into cubicles for rent. Their marble and mahogany reign was finally over. Now was the time of glass towers.

The shortcuts and side streets, too, that had once been shadowy backwaters, romantic and mysterious, had been opened up to the busy day.

Reaching his bench, Martin sat down. There was pain in his chest and in his legs. Sitting very still, he watched the hurrying pedestrians.

Here was life, he told himself; but the thought felt frail and transparent.

Everything had changed and nothing had changed. He had hoped to experience a more abrupt, distinctive return to the world.

Even the news of Marilyn's imminent marriage seldom occurred to him. He imagined she would be happy. Brussels, London. It all felt far away. A June wedding was planned; a quiet ceremony.

Then he recalled the pretty, chilly church where she and he had promised to stay together forever.

Bristol, autumn 1986. Their small gathering: Bill, Josephine and Carmen – Londoners eager only to return to London, barely taking off their coats. His own mother, so touchingly respectable. Piers Harding: an acquaintance from school chance-met just weeks before; impulsively, absurdly, invited to be his best man. Catherine, close to tears, standing next to Marilyn.

Bill had glanced quickly at the order of service, put it down in the pew beside him and then folded his arms across his chest, waiting for something to happen. He disliked Anglicanism, 'for so many reasons,' he said.

Josephine held her prayer book so limply that it fell forward in her hand, unreadable. She made no effort to adjust it.

Carmen rummaged noisily in her bag for something clearly more important to her than the wedding.

Piers, an academic, had performed his single duty with what seemed polite obedience to a quaint but long since refuted concept.

The misty hill, the damp pavement slippery with rust-brown fallen leaves. Tall white houses beyond the dripping trees. The raindrops on parked cars.

Then the moment, quite unexpectedly, when Martin had felt Marilyn's hand take his and realised the immensity of their promises to one another. That had been shortly after the service, outside, beneath the wet autumnal trees. He had just lit a cigarette.

Now, sitting outside the Royal Exchange, he looked around. Here at least were traffic and the City; indifferent to the individual yet somehow trustworthy.

Emil from the office – tall and rangy, in his late forties – had called Martin that morning. Everyone was happy he was up and about; he must be sure to rest and get better.

'And then perhaps we can make a date for you to come in for a chat?'

His quick quiet voice always sounded slightly distracted; always a more pressing matter to attend to.

Not the punk war, not forgetting where you lived, what your job was.

Walking on, Martin felt again – subtle but apparent, would not be denied – that same odd heaviness, forcing him again to stop.

'Well, think what you've been through,' Hannah had said to him the previous evening, when she called him. 'Your body needs time to recover.'

A few days before they had tried going out for supper. Martin looked at the menu and had no appetite. He had wanted to have a drink but the thought of it exhausted him. Happiness was oddly unimaginable.

Hannah looked at him across the table. He was sitting with his head bowed. He looked, she thought, like someone who had lost everything.

'There's some blood on your cuff.'

Martin glanced down at it. 'Yes . . . Sometimes it still bleeds.'

'You know, if you don't feel well you must ring the doctor.'

'I don't know what "well" should feel like. Which is a problem.'

'But surely not how you're looking at the moment?'

'They said it would take a while. And it's been difficult to sleep because whenever I move in bed I tear the cut in my leg.'

Neither a new world nor the old one. What had once been everything and nothing was now neither nor.

★

As Chloe looked towards the big bay window and rainy spring morning beyond, the light in the room was pale grey infused with violet. Turning, craning her neck, the wall behind the bed with its picture rail looked unreal in the half-light. The new day was awake but still dreaming.

Her consciousness had risen from sleep with youthful ease. It was like she could barely wait.

On waking she had felt immense joy before she even remembered why. Opening her eyes she could almost feel their clarity and shine, so eager to take in and take on the world. She was giddily aware of being young, filled with energy and newly, deeply in love.

Beside her, still sleeping, lay Alice; her glorious protectress, lover, older than her, hero-heroine. She whose presence had opened a fourth dimension, hitherto invisible, in which life was filled with meaning, beauty, excitement and joy.

To know she would feel Alice's arms around her, receive her quick dazzling smile, taste her rough or lingering kiss, give in completely to her slow appraising look; make her laugh; drink coffee with her and walk beside her; savour the heavy church incense perfume on her denim jacket.

Now fully awake, Chloe enjoyed the cool white sheets, the yielding depth of the pillows; the close warmth of Alice's body.

She had never felt so joyously and gloriously naked, so open to touch and sensation. To reach the point at which unstoppable kissing and holding and grabbing and stroking brought her to ecstatic abandon, wanting only more. To possess and be possessed by all that contained the very essence of the woman she loved.

Alice woke briefly. She lay on her back with her eyes closed, then pulled Chloe towards her.

'That's where you should be,' she murmured.

Their day lay ahead, luxuriously empty.

The previous evening Alice had asked Chloe to marry her, and Chloe had all but screamed her acceptance.

It was typical of Thomas that he had some dear friends who owned not one but two big apartments on the first floor of an imposing block of mansion flats in Portland Place. The majestic front door was just a few minutes' walk from Regent's Park.

The two properties had been converted to connect, adding a grand dining room to the impressive drawing room. There was also a big kitchen, two staff bedrooms, a study and library, vast master bedroom, a guest suite, three bathrooms and a further reception room at the back with French windows opening onto a balcony that looked west across the rooftops of Marylebone.

The dear friends were seldom, if ever, in London; could not have been more delighted . . .

And so here, with flawless courtesy, charm and good humour, Thomas would hold a lunch party to celebrate his and Marilyn's engagement.

'Will you invite Dad?' Chloe asked her mother when the party was announced. There was a note of reproach in her voice that Marilyn judged rightly to be in Martin's favour.

'Of course. If he'd like to come. If he's well enough. And I'll ask Julian and Paul as well.'

The party would be held towards the end of May.

'It would be nice to get married in Brussels,' Marilyn had said to Thomas, early on in their discussions about the wedding.

'As you like, my dear.'

The agreement was given with the same broad humorous smile – the lovable old clown with the heavy-framed glasses of a television comedian from the days of Marilyn's childhood. Life a pleasant amusement; a wave of the hand, as though to say whatever she wished would be hers.

'And I think it's better that way,' he added. 'Second marriages – forgive me . . .' – he laughed – 'but second marriages are . . .'

'Different to the first one?' Marilyn smiled.

Already she could see in her mind's eye some quiet dignified office in Brussels . . . And this felt right too; privacy and exclusivity. A silent entrance hall in its own twilight; a leather-and-ledger smell of European respectability; art nouveau panelling in carved chestnut.

Brussels, to Marilyn, brought to mind those first pale warm autumn days after the fierce heat of summer.

Then – as far as she was concerned – a small dinner with a few of Thomas's close friends; those older wealthy relaxed men and women who in accepting her as Thomas's second wife would accept her as one of themselves; take away the need for thought, for explanation, for stress of any kind. Make everything easy – as did quiet, efficient, well-paid staff, she was discovering.

And of her own friends . . . Well, Catherine would never feel right in such surroundings; but she must come to the party in London.

Catherine seemed to have a boyfriend now – Richard somebody-or-other. Marilyn was happy for her; relieved she would not have to see her standing alone at another party, somewhat ignored on the edge of a conversation between people more assured than herself; holding her wine glass in front of her chest with both hands. So fatally polite; so ready to join in, if invited.

Yes, Thomas's lunch party would dissolve all sorts of problems, discreetly, firmly; clearing the way for the impeccable, quiet second wedding.

Spring was gathering. The budding trees looked as though they had a green mist hanging in their uppermost branches. The lengthening days became warmer and softer as April gave way to May.

Late one afternoon – it was Thursday, 4 May – Chloe and Alice walked hand in hand from Marble Arch to Kensington Gardens. Each day seemed to deepen their love. Even they could scarcely believe it.

They had told Martin of their decision to get married. He was delighted.

But they would wait until after Marilyn's wedding before they told her.

Chloe and Alice always found it so hard to part. When the moment finally came they stood staring into one another's eyes, unable to stop smiling, nearly laughing; then each would try to walk away, slowly letting go of the other's hand – gradually, gradually, until only their fingertips were touching.

Now there was the familiar bulk of the Royal Albert Hall across the road; the Albert Memorial in sharp black silhouette behind them. The sky had cleared; the dusk was air-force blue. The evening star hung smartly over Lancaster Gate, a tiny flare of dazzling whiteness.

That particular evening, as she walked back to South Kensington station, Chloe was unaware that her father was barely two streets away. He had just arrived at the big lounge-like waiting area of the private hospital on Cromwell Road.

He sat in the corner of a deeply cushioned black leather sofa. On the low glass-topped table before him lay two copies of that day's *Financial Times* and a magazine titled *Chelsea Luxury Leisure*.

At intervals, older patrician or lean young consultants came to collect their patients with a quiet courtesy that gave nothing away. Their ability to cure began with their set smiles, faintly refrigerated charm, expensive ties and brief, quietly uttered greetings.

The previous week Martin had been required to lie very still within the open-ended white tube of a brand-new MRI machine that scanned his heart.

'In immense detail, sectionally,' Dr Howard was now explaining.

Martin always forgot the cardiologist's deep voice; imagined a less formal intonation until they were face to face.

This evening Dr Howard sounded graver than usual. Again, he was looking down at the file, his fingertips pressed together beneath his chin. His tone was emphatic and severe.

'Had you rung me and told me you were still experiencing angina I would have found the prospect almost too remote to take seriously.'

He spoke more to the file than to Martin. 'Which is why I asked you to have this scan, which these days is as accurate as an angiogram – although in my opinion an angiogram remains the gold standard.'

Martin nodded as he might have nodded to a senior master at school who was paying him particular attention.

'I have spoken to David Fox,' the cardiologist continued. 'He's devastated.'

The quiet white-haired surgeon.

For two of Martin's bypass grafts had failed; hence the renewed pain in his chest.

'There are things we can do,' said Dr Howard.

Before him were some sketches in black ink of the patient's coronary situation. He explained them. Martin would return in a fortnight's time to the hospital he had left two months before.

This new information made sense of his recent mood, perhaps.

When he had left hospital the first time the morning had been fresh and bright – winter falling away. The

Surrey trees were still leafless, their boughs black and damp; the air was quick and chill. He had tried to feel in step with the hurrying day.

Returning to London – he recalled his slow walk down Bishopsgate, the first day back; along the broad colonnade that ran above the busy street, up towards Shoreditch; how he had hoped to feel reborn and inspired, aware of latent new strength; but instead was exhausted and short-tempered. Still grimy.

Now, as he left the big hospital on Cromwell Road, Martin sensed the long reach of Thornby Avenue. Something in his destiny, he thought. Cigarettes; cleanliness repulsed – degeneracy. But trying to define the feeling was like struggling to recall the logic of a dream.

Thomas and Marilyn welcomed their guests for lunch on Saturday, 27 May 2017.

The morning was sunny and warm, the sky pale blue. Cherry blossom weather, thought Basil as he strolled up Portland Place. Josephine's oldest friend, he had watched Marilyn grow up. Never forgotten a birthday or Christmas. He had never been quite sure about Martin, but adored Chloe. Snapshots showed him cradling her in his arms when she was just a few weeks old. So unlike him, but there it was.

Today he was dressed in a double-breasted blue suit that still looked quite debonair. With this an ivory-coloured silk shirt and grey silk tie with diagonal stripes of gunmetal and crimson. His jacket lining was a rich damson satin.

That morning, in the tiny bathroom of his flat in Gospel Oak, he had stared at his face in the mirror. He had just finished shaving. However hard he looked, he could never really see himself. A familiar stranger stared back at him. He gave up and splashed his cheeks with Trumper's Eucris.

The address on his invitation card was handwritten – albeit in an unknown hand – the characters swift and jaunty in blue-black ink.

He had asked the taxi to drop him on the corner of Mansfield Street. To walk through London, he always felt, was to walk through the many chapters of his unwritten autobiography.

'My memoirs are walked,' he had said to Martin, twenty years earlier, 'not written.'

Back then, he was not yet sixty. How old they all were now – what was left of the Gang. He and Josephine; and poor Bill, who was finding it difficult to walk.

Basil himself would soon be seventy-nine.

'But I always feel twenty-eight,' he would say to Josephine, as the two of them stood together at one gathering or another, surveying the chattering crowd. The socialites and minglers, their laughter spilling out so easily; still blissfully, proudly at ease with their achievements; yet to notice the shadows lengthening on the lawn.

'Anyway,' he added, 'we've had a fucking good time.'

He had always had more than a soft spot for Marilyn. Carmen he found brash – 'Such a missy' – but Marilyn, so reserved and graceful, so ladylike; with her poise and lovely clothes and that *devastating* smile.

'You should have been in front of the cameras,' he would say to her, nodding earnestly, whenever they met.

He was pleased for her now as he strolled along, looking forward to the party.

Nine days earlier, Martin had sat beside the window in his room at the hospital in Surrey. It looked identical to the room he'd had before; had the same view of a broad grassy verge and the beech hedge that enclosed it.

This time, the cannula was in the back of his hand; and soon he was detached, serene, very still. The delicious surge of coldness in his arm bringing peace. Dr Howard, unfamiliar in surgeon's green scrubs, was standing level to his pelvis.

Martin was conscious but weightless in the pause in time. He felt a sudden warmth below his abdomen.

'Slight tightness coming up,' said Dr Howard, watching the screens.

Another artery widened, Martin was taken back to his room to rest. The following day he was allowed to go home.

'The whole thing,' he said to Hannah that weekend, 'the hospital, the drugs, the technology, everything – it's become a part of me.'

They were sitting on a bench in Victoria Park. Less than two days before he had been floating in the pause in time, surrounded by technology.

'The sedation interrupts your ability to create new memories,' he added.

133

'Ghost in the shell,' said Hannah.

And now, a week later, it was Thomas and Marilyn's lunch party. Drinks at 12.30 p.m. for lunch at 1 p.m.

When Martin arrived he saw Marilyn standing at the far end of the big drawing room – not beside Thomas, who he noticed had glanced at him very quickly when he first walked into the room.

Marilyn was talking to a couple he didn't know. She was laughing at something. Her inclination to stay in the background was gone; her confidence had caught up with her looks.

She was wearing a shirt of vanilla crêpe de Chine, open at the neck, with a fine chain-link pattern of vertical stripes in chocolate-brown outlined in black. The yoke of the shirt had horizontal stripes in the same pattern. With this she wore cream cotton Oxford bags and a pair of tan-and-ivory two-tone brogues, their broad laces pinkish-white ribbons.

Her air of having found happiness, the place where she felt so at ease, was a weight off Martin's mind even after all these years. It was like she had been in training for this new phase all of her life.

Once, perhaps even six months before, he would have felt a surge of longing at the sight of her; to see the expressions and mannerisms he had known and adored, still there through all the years.

Now he could not summon the energy. He wished her well. He felt like someone retiring from a game that had been arduous and exhausting, played deep into the late afternoon – for so much longer and more savagely than anyone had imagined at the exhilarating outset.

The elegant room had been built for nobility and notables. It was filled with light from the two tall windows that looked down into the wide street. Every ornament and furnishing looked valuable, fresh and polished. On a long French sideboard, aggressively modern a century before, two vibrant displays of bright spring flowers burst upwards from a pair of pale-blue vases. Between them stood an antique silver cigarette box.

Carmen caught Martin's eye and waved but did not cross the room to talk to him.

He could see Bill and Josephine sitting on a big sofa in front of the vast marble fireplace. They looked remote, silently in their own world, like twin statues of seated monarchs in a desert. He knew they would be civil to him, but no more than that, even now.

Basil sat facing them in an elegant rosewood chair. He too had looked up when Martin came into the room.

Josephine was watching Marilyn chat with her guests. Martin wondered what she was thinking.

Then, feeling conspicuous, he saw that Thomas was about to come over to speak with him. They had not met before.

Thomas wore immaculate grey flannel trousers, a brown double-breasted jacket, exquisitely tailored to just nip in at the waist, a silver-blue shirt with a very pointed collar and a rust-coloured tie.

'Martin?'

The older man's friendly greeting, hand outstretched. 'I'm so happy to finally meet you – it's great that you were able to come.'

His voice was more accented than Martin had expected; and faster, slightly American at times.

Shaking hands, Martin nodded and gave a slight bow that he hoped seemed personable and good-humoured.

Their brief conversation was a blur of smiles, civilities and pointless laughter. But Thomas was impressive – such confidence, such charm.

'I hope you'll come to Brussels,' he said.

There was a flattering hint of concern in his voice.

'Thank you – I'd like to . . . I always wanted to see the Magritte Museum,' Martin added rather wildly.

'Yes? You're interested in art?'

'Oh, only as a tourist!' Martin felt foolish. 'I'm no expert.' Laughter.

'Well, I don't have a Magritte. But I do have a small early painting by Man Ray. Very small! I'd love you to see it.'

'Oh! How—'

Martin felt immense sadness. His first meeting with Josephine when he was young, besotted with Marilyn and so inexperienced. He had tried to sound cultured, learned – failed abysmally with his first sentence. So eventually, inevitably . . . the colonnade at Bishopsgate; his old black suit; the Polo Bar; '. . . *it is the ease and frequency* . . .'

And Josephine's comment on hearing of his fatal infidelity, 'Well, water finds its own level.'

Before they parted, Thomas held their handshake for a second or two and patted him on the arm, as though the two of them had secured a special relationship – one separate and slightly more important than most.

Martin felt flattered and dealt with, simultaneously.

Two butlers, silent silver-haired men with serious expressions, wearing black ties, black jackets and grey pinstripe trousers, were serving drinks: champagne, sparkling water, Bloody Mary or, for Marilyn – a kiss blown from her fiancé – the 'Cellini' cocktail, this time made with a dash of wild raspberry puree.

Martin realised how badly he wanted a drink. He asked for a glass of champagne.

Then Basil was standing beside him.

'Well, there you are,' he said, regarding Martin with a blank expression.

He seemed to be referring to Martin's first meeting with Thomas. 'He has a Man Ray.' A pert nod accompanied the acknowledgement.

Martin felt he barely knew Basil – but here surely was an ally. Two aliens disguised as humans recognising one another in a crowd.

'I was just thinking . . .' he said.

He could tell from Basil's expression that his tone was too familiar, peculiarly so, but he blundered on.

'. . . about the first time I met Marilyn . . . The first time I saw her, in 1984. It was at the flat of a friend of hers in Chiswick – Catherine. She's here, actually . . . It started to snow just as we were leaving. We

137

watched it falling before we got in her car. Everything seemed so exciting . . .'

He looked for some response, for alien code; that there was none seemed cruel.

'You haven't been well?'

'Oh – it was a little unexpected . . . But when you ask around you realise that everyone's dealing with something.'

The older man didn't reply but his attitude changed, as though the muscles in his face had relaxed.

He guided Martin towards two chairs at the back of the room. They were framed by the hang of sumptuous silver-blue curtains held open with heavily tasselled tiebacks.

'I remember meeting you at the old house in Greenwich.' Basil leant forward, his voice lowered as though he was confiding a secret. 'You were trying far too hard . . . But then, you were rather thrown in the deep end. Josephine's not easy, much as we love her, and Carmen's dreadful. It's never enough for either of them to *win*, socially. Others must be seen to fail.'

These were events from thirty years ago . . . It was all just sad. He hoped the drinks tray would soon reappear. He wondered what Thomas made of Carmen. He imagined that she would detect a slight chill.

Looking up, he saw Marilyn again, across the room, standing beside a table. A succession of guests paused to compliment her. She looked so relaxed, her weight resting on one leg. Her broad shoulders had always made her clothes hang well.

She also looked changed, but in what way? The strong line of her jaw was the same; and the slightly wide face that her smile and dark eyes animated so winningly. Her hair of course was at once so free and easy, yet just so . . . And the way she could rest her hand on your shoulder, so lightly, in a gesture at once humorous, affectionate, fingertips raised . . .

But now she looked rich – that was it; not just well off, in that tasteful yet bourgeois North London way, but noticeably wealthy. She was *in transit* . . . The wholly international life . . . It was suddenly present in everything she did and wore; in her demeanour as much as her aura. She was in London to host a lunch . . .

'She really is beautiful,' said Basil, 'I've always said so.'

Martin nodded and finished off his champagne. Thankfully one of the butlers was heading in their direction, a chilled bottle at the ready, wrapped in a snow-white cloth. Martin held out his glass a little too quickly. The butler's set expression didn't flicker as he poured.

'I suppose the clever word would be "flâneur",' said Basil, suddenly. '"Connoisseur"? No . . . "One who sought transcendence", perhaps.' He raised his eyebrows. 'I only had a minimal education – cleverness never interested me. I was educated by style, and *that* was positively Jesuitical.'

He looked around the room. 'Well, it's better than simply being clever.'

The conversation did not appear to need an interlocutor.

Martin looked at the floor. He wished there was something stronger to drink. He saw again the dark snowy London streets, so quiet; and the following day – the day after he first met Marilyn – there had been a hard frost of the kind that you never seemed to get any more; one of those pink sunsets, very still and silent. He had thought he could hear the ice cracking in the dusk.

Yes . . . He had been to visit his mother; his head so filled with Marilyn. The freezing suburban sunset; the snow and cold and quiet in the fading light; it had felt like a blessing on their romance.

'And the more you think about the past,' Basil went on, 'the more you realise that you're not as nice as you think you are and not as liked as you hoped you were.'

Martin nodded, smiled, said nothing.

'At least you've held down a job,' the older man continued. 'That's something. I had ambitions to be an artist. At eighteen I seemed to be a textbook case. I had the lot – queer, only child, adored Mama, loathed Papa. A loner who had a sense of *the look of things* . . . Would you know who I mean if I mentioned Vuillard? No? Well, never mind . . . I even went to the Slade for about five minutes but I knew before I got there that I'd never be a footnote to a footnote.'

He scanned the room again, his eye resting briefly and judgementally on Thomas. But no comment was forthcoming. 'I sometimes wonder whether Bill will be much more than a footnote. Which is actually rather liberating. Pointless looking to out there' – he gestured with a backwards flick of his hand towards the guests and the grand room – 'for *anything*. The rich are rich, and we're not.'

There was the alien code, surely? Martin was about to reply when he became aware of a sudden commotion behind him.

'Dad!'

Bustle and confusion; then Chloe's radiant smile and laughter.

He turned and felt his daughter's light hand on his shoulder and heavy kiss on his cheek. Then he saw Alice behind her and remembered how much he liked her.

'How are you?' Alice said. 'Chloe told me . . .'

All at once Martin could see the three of them . . . New Year in Switzerland; some blue salon in a spa hotel. The cocktail hour; the snow luminous between the trees.

He turned to look for Basil, to introduce him, but he was nowhere to be seen.

'Where's Mum?' Chloe asked. 'I hope we're sitting near you.'

Marilyn was now standing beside Thomas. They looked so relaxed, so good together. The distinguished humorous Belgian gentleman and his slightly younger, lovely second wife-to-be. Everyone thought it was wonderful. The party had come effortlessly to happy life.

There were twenty guests, maybe half of whom Martin knew. Lunch was announced over chatter and laughter; enthusiastic conversations struck up between people meeting for the first time, acquaintances becoming friends . . . Julian and Paul were in the thick of it, paying great attention to a grand-looking elderly lady, a relative of Thomas's, formerly of New York, now resident in London.

Basil and Josephine were helping Bill to his feet. One of the butlers hurried over to help.

Martin watched the three old people make their way slowly into the dining room. What had Bill once said – some fifties expression?

'. . . we were three old funsters . . .'

But, they had been young and heroic and flippant; as clever as anyone, no strangers to glamour and controversy. The tumbledown white-stucco terraces of Bayswater and Notting Hill, sixty years ago; ciggies and bedsits and high jinks; ancient plumbing, gin and tinned orange juice; '. . . *Red Hot Henry Brown, the hottest man in town . . .*'

Even the Teddy boys outside the pub used to crack a smile at Basil's suggestive twirl, insouciant expression and sudden soft-shoe shuffle; sashaying down to World's End with Josephine.

Then Bill's important conversation and Josephine's opera and significant people; Basil's life of the look of things . . . They had followed a long path through the forest, the three of them, with parties for trees.

The guests took their seats. Marilyn sat at one end of the table, Thomas at the other. A white burgundy was served; Margaux awaited them.

On the far wall, overlooking the long dining table – the attentive butlers just now dipping deftly in and out between the guests – hung a vast eighteenth-century painting; a classical scene: hunters, goddess and nymphs in a glade.

Lunch was sorrel soup, chicken pie and lemon tart.

Nine

The office looked different. Desks had been rearranged and there were new staff Martin didn't recognise. They all looked very young, quiet and studious. Hardly like City types at all. Academics, rather, and the cycling kind who seldom took a lunch break but brought in quinoa-based salads they prepared at home. The one voice he heard was American, speaking very quietly, with barely a pause for breath.

He walked to the place by the window, now empty, where his own desk had stood. Two neat storage boxes made of stout brown cardboard were stacked to one side. He could just make out the imprints of the desk legs in the chemical-scented silvery-grey carpet.

He looked out of the window towards Spitalfields; the white spire of Christ Church; the roof of the market; Julian and Paul's house over to the left. The view from the sixth floor – it always felt like watching a silent film.

The last time he had been in the office – the second week of February; the dark winter evening, cold and raw.

Now it was early afternoon on Monday, 5 June. Another lovely day.

'Martin!'

He turned and saw Emil smiling at him.

'The grand rearrangement,' said Emil with a humorous sweep of his hand.

'I haven't seen a single person I know so far,' said Martin. 'It seems very quiet.'

'Oh, they're all around somewhere. We're having to try out different sections, new teams . . . You know what it's like.'

Martin smiled; knew immediately that his smile was now that of a non-combatant.

'Anyway, come through . . . It's good to see you.'

Tall Emil, fit and lean, his jacket off and shirtsleeves rolled up, led the way into his office. 'Still here!' he remarked, with mock weariness at the sameness of it all.

They took their seats on either side of the desk. Emil seemed unusually attentive. Martin declined an offer of tea, coffee, 'or maybe some water?'

'But how are you? That's the most important thing.'

The line manager leant back in his chair, one long leg crossed lightly over the other. Looking down, he rotated a silver pencil between his thumb and forefinger.

'I'm fine,' said Martin. 'Grateful to—'

'But you had a heart bypass?'

'Yes. It's nothing like as big a deal as it used to be.'

'Even so.' Emil's mouth turned down at the corners; he wore the expression of someone determined never to get anywhere near to having heart surgery.

'I had a check-up not so long ago. It's all basically fine.'

'You're very cool about it.'

'When you ask around you discover that most people are dealing with something.'

The stock response. The democracy of ageing and ailments. So reassuring.

But Emil pulled another long face, held the silver pencil up before his eyes and rotated it slightly faster.

'Well, it's good to see you up and about – thanks for coming in.'

He put down his pencil, looked at his desk and then at Martin.

'I'm guessing you'll probably know what's coming.' Sad smile. 'You're a senior member of the team, in terms of age, so I'd sooner be straight up.'

Martin raised his eyebrows. The saving clause, 'in terms of age . . .', had not gone unnoticed.

'As you can see there are changes going on at all levels. And unfortunately we've had to lose a few people—'

Martin sat very still. The Rolodex spun in his mind, freely and unchecked. A break from the circle . . .

He remembered an overgrown park in Berlin that he had only visited once, with Chloe. A short stretch of still black water, reflecting the trees like a mirror; crumbling stone urns, overgrown with ivy, at either end of a bridge. Chloe would have been about sixteen – shortly to start sixth form. They had sat together on a bench in the quiet with no one else around; agreed the place was special. He wondered if it was still there.

Emil was saying something about the office.

Then Martin saw his old suburban station. There was the bend in the tracks around which the train approached; flanked to one side by big trees; their air of medieval romance.

'Yes,' he said.

'So we'd like to offer you an early retirement package.'

Emil frowned and rummaged through some papers on his cluttered desk. He found two printed sheets stapled together. 'Martin Knight' was handwritten in the top right corner of the covering sheet. He handed them over.

Emil had always managed to camouflage his skills as a corporate team player with the mannerisms of an informal, semi-academic, liberal kind of fellow. But he was not a bad person.

'Actually we're pretty good here, with these kinds of offers,' he was saying. 'Take it away and read it – call with any questions. Any time.'

'But the job?'

'Yeah – I think that's pretty final.'

'Well, thank you. So I'll read it then get back to you.'

Emil stood up, tall behind his desk.

'From a personal point of view we'll all miss you.'

'End of an era,' said Martin as they shook hands.

He turned to leave.

Then, just as he reached the door, Emil said suddenly, 'Do you really care?'

He sounded unusually interested, was smiling but frowning, curious yet momentarily adrift; as though he really wanted to know, to discuss it . . .

Martin glanced at the floor and then shook his head. He didn't know what to say. So he nodded and smiled and made his way towards the lifts.

Nobody looked up or noticed him passing by. He had remained invisible, to the last.

The Indian cigarettes were a rolled brown leaf, tied at their thinner end with scarlet thread. They came not in packets but a pale-pink wrapper, sealed at the top with a densely patterned piece of gummed paper.

Martin, a large gin and tonic before him, could almost smell again the sweetish burning fragrance of the aromatic smoke.

This evening, the evening of Thursday, 8 June 2017, he had let himself fall – luxurious drunken swoon – backwards into the waiting arms of the past.

'No Future', for instance – the roared incantation back then, for types of a certain disposition. Roared in an old rag-and-bone man voice until you retched or ran out of breath . . . In the end, that iconic slogan had conjured neither apocalypse nor anarchy but terminal nostalgia – the most conservative of occupations.

Most of those people had been so messed up anyway. Impossible to be around for long, brewing cyclones of chaos. Locked out at two in the morning, dodging psychotic girlfriends; a lot of drugs.

Martin sipped his drink. As the gin carried him gently towards the weightless pause in time, it seemed to him – a grand emotional significant thought, the drink assured him – as though his reserve and aestheticism had always attracted exhibitionists, addicts, frigid beauties, lonely anarchists . . . extremists of all kinds.

Then 1978 received him. Kew Gardens with Francesca; minor chords, late summer; before he left for university.

Overhead in the bar some song was playing – minor chords again, forty years on; urban nocturne.

'. . . *for real this time* . . .'

The words had a mournful fall. The voice so flat and metallic, far away, despondent – like a message on an old answering machine, left without hope.

'Unarguable.' Martin spoke the word out loud.

He was gorgeously aware of the gale picking up in his head; felt sure he had found the *mot juste*. He reached for his drink; the glass was still pleasingly heavy, the ice cubes knocking softly against the sides.

The high palm trees in the hothouse, like something in a dream; silver smoke in the golden afternoon; electronic music like the sound of a jet descending. His first experience of being adored, but completely; unable to do anything wrong.

Now, across the street, the long grey bulk of Olympia was dark and silent in the orange street light that flooded the warm blue evening. There were no pedestrians and little traffic. Facing the old exhibition hall were red-brick mansion flats; a short parade of shops and cafés, Lebanese, Turkish . . . This part of town, stretching down to Hammersmith from the southern end of Kensington High Street, had always felt remote, forgotten.

For the last hour, in fact, Martin had been sitting in this wine bar, one of just half a dozen customers; content, enjoying himself.

How on earth had he got here? Well anyway, it was all fine.

Dr Howard's one moment of suave levity, voice lowered, confidential, 'Champagne is very good for the arteries, you know.'

Thus Martin had felt authorised and ran with it.

Earlier in the evening he had met Hannah at a restaurant they used to frequent in Fulham. It had barely changed; the décor still proposed an impression, elderly now and faded, of some eternal Côte d'Azur chic: the whole summer ahead – blue sky, seaplane, diving platform; ozone and coconut oil.

Hannah, unusually, had talked about her youth – about when she was seventeen, raised in Camden Town.

After her mother died early one Saturday morning, she said, she went to Selfridges every day – starting that same afternoon. Meandered through the department store's ocean-liner length, concussed and bereft; up to remote departments – banking and travel services; down to perfume and jewellery, then out and on to Marble Arch.

There she had looked through dark glasses – 'I always associated dark glasses with mourning' – across the busy junction and the park that seemed to stretch off like a sea in winter, into nothing but an eventual horizon that stood for some vague afterlife.

'Then I got into fashion. Fashion and books.'

Years before, Hannah and Martin had nearly slept together in a flat in Craven Street.

It was a misty autumn evening, the chill air filled with fine rain. From the window of the tall dark old house you could just see the Strand, the crowds and traffic passing by.

Hannah was lying on the rug, an ashtray before her. 'It was like the most intense, longest-drawn-out one-night stand you can possibly imagine,' she was saying.

'I never had the confidence or the opportunity to have a one-night stand.' Martin sounded distracted, his voice slightly heavy. 'I wish I had. It might have solved all kinds of problems. Only I'd be useless.'

He had craved a cigarette – perilous temptation when drunk. But somehow in that odd musty-smelling flat, on this plain eighteenth-century ghost street that he had never even noticed before – it had felt as though the usual rules didn't apply. That they were through a looking glass; time and tide both different there.

They had been out drinking. Hannah had always been such a good friend to him – and to Marilyn, he had reminded himself.

But he and Marilyn had been having problems. Chloe was at school, not particularly happy; Marilyn always so busy, so well dressed and precise. Their comfortable world had become hardened and brittle.

He had started to feel unwelcome; couldn't see himself any more; had grown apathetic, slightly coarse . . .

He had no idea how or why Hannah was living in Craven Street. She lived mysteriously. It was as though she had just arrived one day and the empty, coldly ministerial property awaited her, arranged by attendant spirits.

The room they were in, for instance, was too big; like an old boardroom cleared of its furniture. A vast expanse of blue carpet; a monumental fireplace of oyster-grey marble, its hearth likewise cleared and carpeted. The fabric blinds on the tall windows had not been lowered. Long white ugly radiators.

Hannah had lit two lamps, but the light didn't reach the corners of the room. Shadows hung like curtains all around them.

'Do you know the most repulsive thing a man has ever said to me?' She took a drag on her cigarette and poured red wine into Martin's glass. 'I was quite young at the time. He said, "Would you mind if I removed your bra as 'twere?"'

She shook her head in disbelief. '. . . "remove your bra as 'twere" . . . "would you mind?" . . .' She repeated the words slowly. 'It was disgusting.'

They had drunk a lot at dinner. One of the old theatre restaurants in Covent Garden; down a steep flight of stairs on a side street, the entrance unmarked.

'It must be 1987,' Martin had said.

'The year we met,' said Hannah. 'You and Marilyn were in that café off Shaftesbury Avenue – the top of

Neal Street somewhere. It was a bar in the evening
. . . I worked there for a while, when it opened. I
don't remember the name. There was a shop upstairs.'

The bustle and clamour of the restaurant had
enfolded them. The moodily fastidious waiters who
adored Hannah – fussed over her, for her extravagant
air and diva demeanour.

Posters for Streisand, Derek Nimmo, George Burns;
a firmament of stars.

So Martin had boarded the roller coaster in the busy
basement diner; show tunes pounded out on an old
upright piano. Hannah across the table, slightly taller
than him and talking about sex.

She had been drinking gin martini and eating steak
tartare. He couldn't quite remember but she had started
to tell him something about how, back in the early
eighties, she used to pick up men in clubs.

'Some days I just woke up in the mood.'

And Martin through heavy red wine had thought of
his own expeditions: Haymarket, the Ritz, 'Suggestion
of Something Special' . . . The memories were trans-
formed by the glorious lift and swoop of his drunkenness into stately and meaningful occasions.

He too had known that sense of urgency. Yes – he
nodded his understanding with blissful seriousness. It
had been as though there was something he had to
do straight away or he would miss something vital,
forever.

And as Hannah had talked about taking casual lovers,
he had remembered her bibliophile tendency.

Some years earlier, '92, '93, sleeping on the sofa at her old flat in Kennington – '*Shit – I've forgotten where I live*' – he had noticed a low, glass-fronted bookcase. The volumes inside were each carefully bound in thick protective cellophane covers, smooth and cool to the touch. Some were quite old, from the 1940s and '50s. One or two had French titles, others were American.

Unable to sleep, he had lit a cigarette and opened one of the books at random. He read the first sentence. It was studiedly, mischievously long; something about whichever of two decisions you made you would regret both.

As they walked back to Craven Street – that unfrequented looming darkness – there had been sudden thunder, the wind picking up.

In the too-big upstairs sitting room with its tall windows looking down into the street, in the circle of golden lamplight, it felt as though they were camping out on a dark ridge, alone, high and remote.

'. . . thinking about what to wear, or not wear,' Hannah was saying. 'I planned everything . . . I actually bought a strap-on . . .'

She'd go to the straighter, rougher clubs; charm some young man – once, a young man and his girlfriend . . . Then they'd go back to her flat. She liked to take photographs . . . The photographs were monochrome. 'I'd take off most of my clothes as well,' she added, leaning with her head against her hand. 'People like being photographed by a nearly naked woman.'

As she was speaking, Martin became startlingly vertiginous. When he looked at the windows or the floor they kept flicking upwards, the horizontal hold of his vision spinning freely.

Hannah was saying, 'There's a moment when—'

Impulsively, he leant over and took her cigarette from between her lips; he took a long drag. Then he gave it back to her, his head swimming even more violently.

She closed her lips around the cigarette; looked up at him as though she was a different person, momentarily undressed, offering herself, wide open.

The wind had grown strong enough to rattle the windows in their frames. Heavy rain sounded like handfuls of small stones being thrown at the panes.

Hannah stood up, tall in the darkness. She was wearing a black singlet and high-waisted black trousers. There was a black jacket over her shoulders; her arms were white in the shadows. She opened one of the windows. It made a tremendous noise as she raised the sash, like a rusty chain being dragged across a concrete floor.

Martin pulled himself up, unsteadily, then stood beside her, feeling the cold damp air on his face. He closed his eyes. The falling sensation returned immediately and more intensely. He staggered against her bare arm. His hand brushed the waistband of her trousers, clumsily.

'Sorry . . .'

The back of his shirt was damp with sweat.

He was nearly in the wreckage of the roller coaster. But for a few minutes more the carriage rolled along, taking the bends. They might get away with it yet; even though the walls were rolling over his head and he could feel his face soaring up into the ceiling.

Hannah's reminiscences; fun in her flat with boys and girls. The words came back to him, vivid and persistent.

Then Hannah herself had returned. A triangle of light stretched over the carpet.

Somewhere in his head a snowy mountain path had just disappeared; as had the scene her words had conjured. Her old flat . . . Kennington, Oval . . . The room at the front had pale-yellow walls; the glass-fronted bookcase. In his mind's eye he glimpsed a summer sunset over a concrete wall; the camera she had . . .

Then the old house on Craven Street had been cold, dark, empty and unfriendly.

In the years that followed, neither of them discussed that evening. Just let it fall away; nothing to say. It was very odd, the whole experience . . . Not like them at all. Supernatural things happened in London all the time . . . And Hannah would have gone through with it, Martin felt sure. And despite the Polo Bar, despite everything, he was glad that—

'What are your plans?' Hannah had asked, just an hour ago.

'I have absolutely no idea.'

'Maybe take some time to think your own thoughts.'

'I suppose so.'

Their dinner seemed a long time ago – how many drinks? They must have met early. They had walked to Knightsbridge in the blue midsummer evening. The windows of the high-fashion shops made Martin think of foreign cities; prosperous Europe, endless. Milan, Salzburg, Munich, Vienna. Everywhere, in fact. Bark-brown and dulled gold; marble lobbies. Fendi perfume.

He supposed that was the world that Marilyn would enjoy.

Pleasantly drunk, suddenly inspired by the road towards Olympia, he had decided to stay out.

'You're sure you're okay?' Hannah hailed a cab and dropped her cigarette into the gutter. 'For Christ's sake, don't push it. You know you have to be careful?'

'I'm fine. I've had a nice evening.' He looked again down the blue street. 'West London – it's a funny old place.'

Hannah kissed him on the cheek and got into her cab.

Twenty minutes later Martin had ordered another drink and was surveying his surroundings.

Fifty years ago this whole area had been quite bohemian. Young men with long hair and panda-eyed girls who worked in boutiques or went to art college; fiddling around with portfolios and front-door keys and calling it freedom.

Now, such quiet; no one much about. Martin tried to pay attention to his future as a retired man.

'Gareth had this notion,' Chris Menzies had once said to him, 'that if he could just get home, back to his mother's house, then he'd be alright.'

'How so?'

'He thought everything he knew would simply be waiting for him. And he'd be a teenager again and he'd be well. He was looking for a time machine. But his liver was totally shot.'

The train windows had been streaked with heavy rain. Low clouds over a delta of tracks; distant flats in the mist.

They had been to Gareth's memorial service. Chris was a college acquaintance, burly, decent. He looked like a builder. Martin had been glad that he was there.

It was a strange occasion – all awry. Held near a ring road on the outskirts of Croydon known locally as the Berlin Wall.

The damp grey afternoon came into Martin's mind. Late nineties.

A nervous young man who wore a belted brown raincoat over his suit had given a eulogy of sorts – some film about deep-sea diving; there in a draughty hall with a random view across a mean strip of car park. It had looked like a room where riot police were briefed.

And Gareth's mother sitting outside afterwards. A big woman, wearing a knitted shawl; black hair, inconsolable; her face in her hands. The only place to sit had been on a low corrugated-steel crash barrier.

Next day, the bright morning sunshine pressed hard against Martin's lowered blind and woke him, dyspeptic and anxious, all but under the thumb of dread.

He remembered leaving Olympia in a cab – speaking volubly with the driver about London changing; had parted on good terms, certain of all the poetry and meaning and affability in the world, in all of London, all of East London.

Now there was nothing; that magical world had dropped away. The poetry and meaning, insights and glad speculations – all had disappeared. Nothing was favoured; nothing but tiredness and sickness and sour thoughts remained.

There was the harsh light on the windowsill. Martin, feeling grimy, covered in sweat, felt his heart racing. However he lay in bed, the closeting safety of night long gone, the clean world long up and about, busy, content and full of good purpose, he, the drunk, could not even find rest.

Not that these feelings were in any way new. They had become part of the contract – the principal deal in his life. To weigh the pleasures of the night's drinking against their consequences. Only now – the vertical scar down his chest; the others down the inside of his left leg and underside of his left forearm.

Madness.

He swung his legs out of bed and sat for a moment, his head bowed. Before him the lowered blind barely held back the bright morning light.

His day was gone already, its promise cleared out. It had been one of those nights when he did not fall asleep but lost consciousness, suddenly.

He opened his eyes again and raised his chin; stared

at the blind. He was aware of the light behind him falling from the kitchen into the windowless hallway.

On the shelf above his bed stood a silver-framed photograph of Chloe; her exuberant expression, laughing. Maybe now he didn't have a job they could go back to that park.

Yes. Time for a change, maybe. Stuart had stopped, after all. As far as he knew.

A few hours later Marilyn was parking her car. She had been to see George, her hairdresser, and if she was going to meet Thomas at the Eurostar she would have to hurry. She ran quickly into the house to change her shoes and pick up her bag.

She was just upstairs trying to decide which jersey to take – it was only a weekend trip and the weather was so fine – when she heard the doorbell.

Glancing at her watch she hurried downstairs. Twenty past one. In the hall she adjusted one of her earrings. It had been bothering her all morning. Another ring. She opened the front door.

There were two police officers – a man and a woman.

'Marilyn Fuller?' The male officer was young, bearded. He glanced very quickly at a sheet on the clipboard he was holding.

'Yes?'

'May we come in, please?'

Marilyn felt her heart beat faster. She noticed the female officer, short and blonde, was looking at her rather oddly.

Without thinking Marilyn sat down suddenly on the small chair in the hall. Hands on her knees; like when Martin . . .

The young man took a breath.

'I have some very bad news I must tell you.' He spoke slowly, in a level voice, not taking his eyes off her. 'Your daughter has been involved in a traffic accident and I'm sorry to tell you that she has died.'

For a second or two Marilyn stared at him, not understanding; then she felt her left arm hit the wall with violent force and fell blindly to one side.

Ten

The white coffin passed by Martin and Marilyn so close they could have touched it. Marilyn squeezed Martin's hand, tighter, tighter.

There was a spray of pale-pink roses on the coffin lid. Marilyn only managed to look once, her shining eyes staring in horrified disbelief.

Alice was one of the pallbearers, dressed in black, her face very pale.

A week before, she had told Martin and Marilyn that Chloe had wanted to be dressed in Dior on her wedding day. Marilyn looked up, as though someone had done her a great kindness.

'We'd love that.' Her voice was very quiet. 'Thank you. Yes.'

So Alice had bought Chloe's funeral clothes in New Bond Street, pretending she was a personal assistant selecting an outfit for her boss; never once losing her composure. The white double-breasted Bar jacket and matching pleated calf-length skirt in white tulle; pink crystal heels from the new collection.

In Chloe's room in Putney, that same afternoon, she sprayed her perfume over the garments before she took them to the undertaker's, wrapped in fine black tissue paper in their big glossy carrier bag.

There were Chloe's bed sheets, still rumpled as she had left them; her small collection of books; some postcards she had saved. An illustration, silvery grey – *The Serpentine Is a Lovely Lake.*

At the undertaker's Alice had felt like a mother leaving a change of clothes at the school for her child. The gentle assistant took them from her – a kindly woman, neither young nor old, softly spoken. A go-between for the dead. Then Alice left quickly, with the set expression and determined stride that Chloe had found so bewitching.

She fumbled for a cigarette in her jacket pocket. A little way down the street she leant against the wall, lit up with trembling hands and stared at the pale-blue sky.

Thomas had given the cost of the outfit to a charity.

Two days later Alice visited Chloe for the last time.

From across the dimly lit room she looked as if she was in a very deep sleep. So pretty.

'Oh darling – darling . . . What have you done? I love you. Oh I love you so much . . .'

The words came without thought; in her head, then half-spoken. That Chloe was so close, so real, so herself, but gone away.

Then Alice became aware of the pallor and profound stillness; the line of Chloe's dark eyelashes; the fresh young cheeks already slightly dark and hollowed.

They had used her own lipstick — it had been in her bag when she died; a new pinkish shade she had just bought.

Then Alice could not bear what she was seeing. Her keening heart; her living love for Chloe felt like a flare in immense darkness.

They had been together that last sunny morning, just outside Hammersmith station; but Alice by chance had crossed the road first — had not seen the accident. Worse, she had heard it. A sudden loud gasp from the people crowded on the pavement, immediately followed by cries of disbelief. A uselessly blared horn.

Alice had turned to ask Chloe what was going on but could not see her.

Two months on, the rooftops of London were shimmering in the heavy heat of August; a haze over the city.

Towards midday — a Wednesday — the Underground train had just left Queensway station. Martin was sitting halfway down a nearly empty carriage.

He was going to Holland Park.

There was an interview for a part-time job; an elderly lady, a friend of Paul and Julian . . . Very kind.

Martin wasn't even sure he would turn up. He just wanted to keep moving.

As usual he had woken early. It was important — Diane, his new therapist, had stressed this — for him to have something to do, a structure to the day.

Since Chloe — something had happened to him. He wasn't sure what. He had been given different explanations by well-meaning people. People who were experts; people who had compared his situation to others they had known, even to their own experience.

To all of them he had turned a gentle smile. He would nod, frowning slightly to indicate how helpful he felt they had been and to thank them; he would say, 'Yes' or 'I see.' He spoke softly, was extremely polite.

But something had happened to his throat and to the way that he breathed. It was difficult. He could manage if he didn't think about it; but if he was caught unawares, if he tried to speak without preparing himself, it became a problem. He had seen a very sympathetic doctor. There was no physiological trouble, he was told; his airways were not constricted; his heart was beating normally. Shock of course could be . . .

Almost every night from six thirty onwards he drank gin; sitting beside the kitchen table in the same chair, staring out of the long window towards some far-away tower blocks. The summer night sky was charcoal streaked with gold; then blue, deeper and deeper; the high stars beyond number.

Marilyn was in Switzerland with Thomas, the last he had heard.

Martin was always stilled within the centre of himself; wanting to sit motionless. In the evenings the gin brought stillness – most times. During the day he felt more at ease travelling around the city. And he was always thinking; but if he tried to speak—

The world – the world of Thomas and Marilyn's engagement party, or his evenings with Hannah – had disappeared. Not those particular activities, but his sense of a place, anywhere, that was not his motionless world. It was like the old philosophical riddle: whether something was there when you couldn't see it. Martin saw a world vividly, in his head. Nowhere existed save his thoughts, which were formless, and what he could see around himself.

Thinking back, it was as the coffin passed by that the stillness had entered into him. He had watched the steady procession; descended deeper and deeper into himself; heard Basil behind him, trying to stifle his tears in the silence that followed.

The big fashionable church in Paddington, arranged by Thomas. Ornate circular windows high above the aisle and nave.

Helpless, they had brought their grief into the building – carried it in with the coffin. It was as though they had nowhere else to go.

Now the Underground train rattled on with a roaring sound. Unsure of where they were, Martin looked up.

Across the carriage, slightly diagonal to him, a woman a little younger than himself was staring into space, deep in her own thoughts. Suddenly her eyes met Martin's and she smiled.

'Miles away,' she said.

She had dark skin and her shoulder-length black hair was braided, showing her fine, high forehead.

Her eyes were set slightly wide apart and when she smiled her pretty face was filled with warmth. She was in her forties, maybe fifty.

On that hot day she wore a long linen skirt and a white cotton shirt, open over a black sports vest. Her sunglasses were pushed back on her head. Her canvas bag was beside her feet.

It was very curious, then quickly alarming. For as she spoke, the stillness in Martin came alive – stiffened suddenly, causing his shoulders to shake. His breath came in broken gasps. He could tell that the woman was looking at him.

He stood up, trying to smile. His chin and jaw felt awkward, violently trembling. His body shuddered, beyond his control.

The train arrived at Holland Park. Leaning heavily with one hand against the opened doors he stepped unsteadily down onto the long platform.

The train rattled and roared away. After it left there was no one else in sight. His eyes tightly closed, Martin leant with his hands pressed against the wall, trying to get his breath.

He felt a hand on his shoulder.

'Are you—'

Turning, he saw the woman who had been sitting across from him.

'You don't look well.' Her voice was very calm.

Martin closed his eyes again and shook his head.

'Come and sit down – come to the bench.'

She guided Martin a few steps. His shoulders shook

and he had to breathe through his open mouth, almost panting.

Then he stopped. It was as though his contact with the stranger had touched a hair-fine trigger, tense and sensitive, long hidden deep inside him.

That was how it began: the air seeming stuck in his throat, yet pushing ever upwards as he tried to breathe in gasps, incapable of speech – until finally, leaning towards the woman, the cry that he had wrestled with for so long broke free from within him.

The tears flowed freely, his face creased tight with sorrow; and Martin let out a choking sob that filled the cavernous silence of the empty platform. Then another fast behind it and another, his voice trying to shape a word but managing only broken panted sounds.

He realised he was holding the stranger's arms very tightly and loosened his grasp, shaking his head. Still his choking tears would only allow his breath and voice to come in gasps. Holding his arm, the woman took him the last few steps to the bench. He sat down heavily and covered his face with his hands.

The paroxysms were easing very slightly and what had been only a guttural sound was slowly becoming a word. Then, every time the word was on the point of forming, the gasping sobs overtook him again and the hot tears and the look of utter despair and panic in his eyes, of all hope lost.

He felt the woman's hand on his back. She was still calm, sitting patiently, watching him.

'Take your time,' she said.

She realised that he was trying to say 'My daughter.'

'What about your daughter?' The woman's voice was gentle.

'Dead.'

Martin stared at her with red, streaming eyes, helpless.

The woman let out a low moan of sorrow. She shook her head.

'How long?'

'Two months ago . . .' He struggled with the words. 'She was twenty-six . . .' And then his face screwed up again, and he covered his eyes with his hand.

'Oh, I am so sorry. Oh – that is sad, so sad.'

Martin tried to recover his breath. Another Tube train came and went.

The minutes passed, then his shoulders slumped and his hands felt limp. He took some deeper breaths. His chest felt more open.

He made a useless gesture with his hands, as if to say he had no decent explanation for his behaviour.

'You've been very kind.'

He shook his head again; took another breath, wiping his eyes. 'I really hope I didn't alarm you. It's been—'

The woman moved away, her hands folded in her lap.

'My name's Ayan.'

'Martin.'

'It's nice to meet you, Martin.'

They shook hands.

'Are you going to be okay?'

'Of course, yes. I'm fine. Thank you, really.'

'You don't need to thank me.'

They stood up. The woman was looking in her bag.

'It might do you good to talk.' She gave him a folded slip of glossy paper. There was a photograph on one side of a waterfall.

'Thank you.'

'Up to you,' she said. 'You're always welcome.' She lifted her bag onto her shoulder, then squeezed his arm.

She turned and walked away, casually, unhurried.

Martin walked slowly down the platform in the other direction. He wanted to wait a few minutes. It would have felt wrong to see her again.

Then it was as though the tightness around his hand, where Marilyn had gripped it so hard, had finally dissolved. But now he could feel a slight warmth on his back – the imprint of the woman's hand or the illusion of it.

He sat down on a bench further up the platform, exhausted. Worn out, he stared across the tracks towards an empty grey space where an advertisement had been. He let out a deep breath.

He felt the folded sheet of paper in his pocket. He took it out and looked at it. On one side, the photograph of a vast waterfall, surrounded by meadows and mountains. Of course. Evangelical maybe. On the other side was a quotation:

He will wipe away every tear from their eyes and death shall be no more, neither shall there be mourning, nor crying, nor pain any more, for the former things have passed away. (Revelation 21:4)

Martin put the paper back in his pocket. Then he slowly got up and walked back down the platform.

Supernatural things happened in London all the time. So Martin had often reminded himself, over the years.

Some of these events were more overt; others occurred as if on the edge of your vision, almost out of sight.

He kept the sheet the woman, Ayan, had given him. It became like a secret he looked forward to thinking about, to studying. He turned the encounter over in his mind. When he was drunk it felt alive, surrounding him; true.

But that was the gale in his head, he told himself. Arms folded tightly across his chest, blissful rocking on the bench by Bank station in the cold; the restaurant for clerks on Carter Lane; a Christmas tree decked with playing cards.

Summer passed quickly into autumn. Tranquil days of warm sunshine, the limp leaves dusty and tired; giving way to the change of season's sudden exhilaration. Soaring and roaring days of blue sky, the wind tearing through the tops of the trees.

One evening in early October, Hannah and Martin went for dinner at Julian and Paul's house in Spitalfields.

The two men were waiting in the big hallway to greet them. They both looked pale and anxious in the dim golden light. It was the first time that Martin had seen them since the funeral.

Conversation was difficult.

'Maybe it's too soon,' said Julian, later, as the four of them sat in the upstairs sitting room. The busy promenading Viennese looked down on them from their painted blustery world. Their adjudicating stare felt brutal.

'Have you heard from Marilyn?' asked Martin.

'I spoke to her once. She sounded better than I expected. She just says it will take a very long time – that she won't get over it. But she didn't say a lot. You know what she's like. Sometimes it's hard to really know what she's thinking.'

Martin remembered the quiet young woman, more like a pensive girl, who had lain on his bed in Vauxhall, stroking his arm, believing in him utterly.

Early one evening a few weeks later, Martin went to a meeting in a church in Shoreditch.

He had always found the building impressive. English baroque; majestic, dilapidated.

There were more people than he had expected. A circle of old stack chairs with grey plastic seats.

He had had a few drinks and was suddenly worried that he must smell of alcohol or – to those who recognised the telltale signs – be obviously half drunk. The suddenly slurred or mispronounced

173

word; excessive friendliness – being too nice, too earnestly interested . . .

So he took his seat slightly apart, wearing a severe expression. Mature respectability. Even so he felt conspicuous, sitting there in his black overcoat.

A white-haired older man introduced the meeting. He spoke about feeling lost in the world, lost in your life – that this was the modern condition.

When he looked around the circle of strangers, Martin felt his throat tighten, the tears well up again. He stared down at the floor and pushed his emotion down, hard, back into himself.

He wanted to tell them about his wedding day and how it had all felt strange and wrong; about Gareth's desolate memorial service; the panic-stricken singer pointing to the side of his head. About the years he had spent in restaurants and bars; the welcoming dark-ness, the drinks and the blissful gale in his head, being weightless in a pause in time, on the roller coaster . . .

He wished he could bring it all into the old church, with its towering pillars and high arched windows and ancient pews; the regal and the derelict – into this coldly lit gathering of strangers. The racing years, lately drunken and soaring; the wicker chest in a sunbeam. Marilyn and Chloe and Alice; the luminous snow between the pines . . . Everything that had brought him here.

A younger man spoke. He had short dark hair and very piercing blue eyes. Dressed in jeans and a black-and-white tracksuit top, he leant forward with his elbows on his knees. He might have been a football coach. His voice was low and fast; an East London accent.

Martin tried to follow what he was saying. He felt distracted and anxious. He wanted to speak and he wanted to leave.

The young man was saying, '. . . and something brought you here—'

Soon after this the meeting dispersed. Martin walked slowly towards the old side door and dark street beyond. He felt the chill air on his face, could smell the rain.

Martin had accepted Emil's early retirement offer. As the line manager had said, it wasn't such a bad deal.

'Well, you've put in the hours,' said Hannah. 'Year after year.'

He saw the bend in the tracks; the tall trees with their medieval air.

One mild autumn day he went to London Bridge station and boarded the train back to his old suburb.

The train set off beneath immense sky. Gradually on either side the city thinned out into suburbs; streets and flats gave way to parks and houses; shabby terraces alternated with elegantly restored villas.

Mostly, the world of the railway; stairs and foot-bridges, low metal benches.

Eventually, the landscape acquired what felt like a certain innocence, distinct from the city's unpredictable vastness. Much had changed since Martin's suburban youth – but less than he had imagined.

He recalled the elevated tracks in East London, the familiar vista. He wondered whether he wanted to return there – to grow old there.

Bishopsgate, Bank and Moorgate no longer felt like his world. His time in the City was over; as if one quite ordinary day he had crossed some invisible border and disappeared in an instant, like he had walked out of shot – gone from the busy streets.

The bright modern train reached his old station. Martin saw that the three big chestnut trees were still standing; and there was the little kiosk – now turned into an espresso bar – where the senior commuters of his youth used to buy their newspapers. '*FT* and *Telegraph*, please.' The old officer class.

He walked through the subway with its smell of damp; then down two short well-known streets. Really, not that much had changed.

'Gareth had this notion that if he could just . . .'

And the flat was actually quite nice. Brand new, top floor – the second floor – with a big sitting room, bright kitchen, decent-sized bedroom. It was one of the two largest, in fact, in this latest conversion to residential use of what had once been the London suburban offices of a French-owned insurance company . . .

Martin remembered the building going up in the early nineties. It stood on a road near the busy little cluster of shops – two restaurants now as well, he noticed – that the locals of Thornby Avenue called the Village.

There was even a small roof terrace outside the big sitting room, with a view towards the dark line of trees where the Heath began – that tract of romantic wilderness that marked the edge of London and beyond which, to Martin, lay some unknowable elsewhere.

Because the flats were being marketed to retired people, the agent was an older man who spoke of comfort, respectability and convenience.

'You don't want to find some bloody rock group living next door,' he had joked.

Martin leant on the windowsill of the big newly painted empty room, looking out.

'You can't rent in Hackney all your life,' Hannah had said. 'Cities change. It costs a lot to keep up with them. More than most of us have.'

He gazed at the view. The autumn afternoon was still and warm – so familiar. The undersides of the clouds were like low white waves, gently rolling to a placid shore above the treetops.

There was a pause in time, neither distant nor sudden, but the start of a beginning. The former things had passed away.

And he could tell Hannah about it. That would be alright. He could talk to Hannah. She would understand.

Acknowledgements

The author would like to thank Lee Brackstone, Polly Braden, Silvia Crompton, Georgia Goodall, Antony Harwood and Donna Huddleston.

Credits

White Rabbit would like to thank everyone at Orion who worked on the publication of *Unfinished Business*.

Agent
Anthony Harwood

Editor
Lee Brackstone

Copy-editor
Silvia Crompton

Proofreader
Seán Costello

Editorial Management
Georgia Goodall
Alice Graham
Jane Hughes

Charlie Panayiotou
Tamara Morriss
Claire Boyle

Audio
Paul Stark
Jake Alderson
Georgina Cutler

Contracts
Dan Herron
Ellie Bowker
Alyx Hurst

Design
Nick Shah

Tomás Almeida
Joanna Ridley
Helen Ewing

Finance
Nick Gibson
Jasdip Nandra
Sue Baker
Tom Costello

Inventory
Jo Jacobs
Dan Stevens

Production
Katie Horrocks

Marketing
Lindsay Terrell

Publicity
Ellen Turner

Sales
Jen Wilson
Victoria Laws
Esther Waters
Group Sales teams
across Digital, Field,
International and
Non-Trade

Operations
Group Sales Operations
team

Rights
Rebecca Folland
Alice Cottrell
Ruth Blakemore
Ayesha Kinley
Marie Henckel